African Eyes

African Eyes

Janette A. Rucker

Copyright © 2015 by Janette A. Rucker.

ISBN:	Softcover	978-1-5035-5369-9
	eBook	978-1-5035-5368-2

All rights reserved. No part of this book may be reproduced or transmitted in any form or by any means, electronic or mechanical, including photocopying, recording, or by any information storage and retrieval system, without permission in writing from the copyright owner.

This is a work of fiction. Names, characters, places and incidents either are the product of the author's imagination or are used fictitiously, and any resemblance to any actual persons, living or dead, events, or locales is entirely coincidental.

Any people depicted in stock imagery provided by Thinkstock are models, and such images are being used for illustrative purposes only.
Certain stock imagery © Thinkstock.

Print information available on the last page.

Rev. date: 04/06/2015

To order additional copies of this book, contact:
Xlibris
1-888-795-4274
www.Xlibris.com
Orders@Xlibris.com
709336

ABOUT THE BOOK

This book African Eyes is just one of my mission statements. When I would read and look at stories about the Africans and the slaves and how they lived and struggled and seen how hard it was for them it would really mess me up. I would wonder how we as people now could endure their pain and know what we know now as we look back there. I wondered how the slaves would adjust and live in this time with all this opportunity and freedom and what would they think of us as the new African people and how we live and adjust to this new way of life. Can you just imagine and just see the tears flowing from their eyes to see people like President Obama and Oprah running stuff!! Just to see their face watching our people come up so far but then how some have went down so far. I often wondered so I wrote this book and I hope you enjoy it.

I first like to thank God for all he keeps doing for me in my life. Thanks to my wonderful dad who left me with the joy of knowing and having a good father. Thanks to my awesome mom for always being there in my life all 55 years. I am sending out thanks to my brothers and sister Earl, Michael Jerry and Linda Andrews for putting up with your sis. To my church family I thank you for keeping my shoulders up when I was down and to the rest of my family and in laws I love you all so much. I would also like to thank the people out there that have been reading my books and encouraging me to keep on, I so appreciate it and last but surly not least thank you Robert Lee Rucker for giving me half your life and supporting me and taking care of me. I love you so much hubby. Thanks peace and love. Janette Rucker "Carol" God Bless you all.

CONTENTS

CHAPTER ONE   BECOMING A MAN 1

CHAPTER TWO   HELL ON WATER 8

CHAPTER THREE   THE BIG HOUSE 15

CHAPTER FOUR   THE HOUSE NIGGER 20

CHAPTER FIVE   A CHANCE TO LIVE 27

CHAPTER SIX   TO LIVE AND NOT LOVE IS DEATH 33

CHAPTER SEVEN   A GHOST FROM THE PAST 41

CHAPTER EIGHT   THE NEW AFRICA 46

CHAPTER NINE   THE BLACK WOMANS DRAMA 50

CHAPTER TEN   RASING A GROWN MAN 58

CHAPTER ELEVEN   COTTON FIELDS TO JAIL HOUSE 66

CHAPTER TWELVE   HAIL THE NEW CHIEF! ...:................. 75

CHAPTER ONE

BECOMING A MAN

The tears fell down Tomba's face as he heard the announcer introduce to the huge Chicago arena the next President of the United States. The black man stood tall and proud as he accepted all the applaud from the people who were all excited and happy with the announcement. Tomba a six foot dark black strong built man with no hair on his head and sparkling white teeth watched all the people of different nationality all in unison, all with different struggles but now all together as one, jumping up and down, laughing crying but no one was more happier than Tomba because this was history and he knew history more than anyone. To look at Tomba he looked like an average forty year old man but looks can be deceiving and only he knew the difference. This is his story.

 Tomba's story is a strange magical one, it didn't start forty years ago, no it starts back in the 18oos. Tomba was a young African boy of eighteen he and his parents lived in a small tribe in Kenya. His father Sekelaga was the chief of the tribe he had a mother Wesesa and a small brother Aiyetoro that was fifteen years old. Tomba was happy he had no worries or troubles the tribe had about three hundred people. There was many huts in the village and all the men wore lion skin cloths around their waist while the women all shapes and sizes wore their cloths covering their treasures. There were fathers and mothers and children all happy all living in peace and harmony under the watchful eye of the Chief Sekelaga. Wesesa was so proud of her husband and her sons who were growing older and ready for manhood. Tomba was the oldest so Sekelaga his father had a watchful eye out for him because one day he would sit as Chief of the tribe and the people loved and respected the Chief because of how he took care of everything and he wanted his son to be able to have that same kind of love and respect. The first step was the trial to manhood.

Tomba along with the other young men sat around one night around the fire as the Chief and the elders talked with them about the trials they had to take to become a man and the journey they had to take. The young men listened because they knew if they didn't complete the task they would have to wait until next year when the flowers bloomed again. No one wanted to fail and be looked down at. The mission for the boys was to take a long fifty mile journey that had traps and animals in the hot sun to the highest mountain, climb it and bring a special flower grown up there and bring it back and present it to the young woman that was chosen for them to marry. Every son had a young woman picked out for them, this was the tradition and very special for both the man and the woman because not only would he be considered a man and be able to move out on his own to his own hut he would also be able to have his mate and at this time in the fellows lives the hormones was high and the young men were ready to leave their families nest and start their own families. Tomba was ready and excited because he being the Chief's son and the next in line to run the tribe he got first pick. Asante was the young woman he had his father picked out for him.

Asante was the most beautiful young woman in the village she was a dark skin smooth face young woman with short nappy hair her body was curvy and she had long beautiful legs and big brown eyes that sparkled every time she looked at Tomba. Tomba and Asante had grew up together, Asante's father was one of the elders of the tribe and a long time friend to the Chief and when they were young children, both families had destined these two to be as one and it didn't hurt that they were in love. Tomba sat and listen as his father told all the young men about the journey and to watch for all the traps set for the vicious animals. Tomba knew of many of the young men that didn't make it back, either falling in the holes that was set up or being eating by the lions the traps was set for, but this was a mission he had to take not only to be Chief and to make his mother and father proud but to be a man and be on his own and marry Asante. After the meeting was done all the young men left to go back to their huts to talk to their families and rest up for the morning journey but Tomba slipped away to Asante's hut and made an animal sound to get her to come out, Asante's mother knew that Tomba was outside and this was his way to sneak and see Asante. Asante's mother smiled when Asante said she had to go out and relieve herself. Asante's mother was just happy her daughter was getting a good man and she would be a Chief's wife one day. Asante left the hut then walked toward the trees in the jungle among the tall grass and saw Tomba waiting for her. Tomba smiled at his future mate who ran over to him and grabbed both his hands and then they stood there just holding hands and smiling at the sight of each other.

"*Tomorrow I will leave as a young boy but I will come back a man, ready to join with you and start our family.*" Tomba said "*And I will be waiting for you to come back to me and I will be proud to be your mate and have your babies and grow old with you together forever.*" Asante said and smiled at her future mate. They both talked more of the arrangement of their living together. Tomba had already got the hut and Asante had it all fixed up and filled with water and food. "*Asante, my beautiful Asante tonight I go back to my families hut and the next few I'll be on my journey but the night after that I hope to be laying next to you my love.*" "*And I also wait for that night and all the nights after to lay next to you my love.*" Asante said as they both looked deep into each others eyes then Tomba told Asante he had to leave before her father got back from the meeting with the elders. Tomba didn't want to disrespect his future family, then he walked Asante back to her hut. There were no kisses or hugs because their tradition was you had to be as one before you showed that sort of affection to one another.

Their village was a peaceful one and any small squabbles the Chief would handle them fairly. Everyone had about the same, their own hut and food to eat, no one was too rich or too poor. There wasn't any baby mama's and daddy dramas, all babies born were raised by both parents and they were together. The people respected each other and followed the tradition establish that made their village good, and Tomba was going to keep it that way, so he said his goodbye to Asante and went back to his family's hut. When Tomba got there the Chief his father was waiting for him outside the hut. "*Sorry father, I'm late getting back I wanted to…*" "*Stop son I know where you were, you had to go see your* woman before you take out on your long journey, it is fine son. I did the same thing with your mother, it gives you power to succeed when you know what you got waiting for you when you return." The Chief said and smiled then he patted his son on the back then he got serious and told Tomba all the things to look out for on this mission, because he was concerned not just as a Chief but as a father. *"Don't worry father I am your son, not only will I be back but I will be the first one."* Tomba said proudly. The Chief hugged his son and they both entered the small hut where Tomba's mother, and his younger brother Aiyetoro was there waiting for the Chief and Tomba to get there so they could eat. After a big dinner that Wesesa fixed, that was all Tomba's favorite dishes the family sat around and talked. Aiyetoro suggested that he wished he could go along with his brother on the trial. *"Don't worry next season it will be your time, Aiyetoro, every boy has to take their own journey to manhood."* *"Yes father only Tomba is not so interested in the journey he just can't hold out any longer waiting for Asante!"* Aiyetoro laughed. Tomba laughed with him embarrassed because it was a lot of truth to what his brother said, proving to be a man was important, but mating with Asante meant much more. The family talked more then they all laid down to sleep.

The next morning the whole village was up to see the young men off. There were ten young men going on the quest of manhood. Tomba could see the fear in some of their eyes as this was a dangerous journey, but one they all had to take. Tomba's family along with Asante stood there smiling and quietly praying to God that Tomba would return home safe. Chief Sekelaga said the last few words to the men then gave the nod for the journey to begin. The men took off running with all their accessories, water food, blankets and their spears attached to them. The Chief smiled as he watched Tomba walk slowly knowing that this would be a long journey and he told Tomba don't let your mind try to out run your legs it wont happen, because your legs will say no, they both need to rest and think. Too bad the other young men didn't know that, so they ran as fast and as long as they could until most of the young fellows got tired and had to stop while Tomba paced himself.

After hours of walking in the hot sun Tomba finally got to the jungle area he had to go through to get to the mountain. Tomba saw the dead caucus of the animals that had been eaten by the lions and prayed he wouldn't be their next supper. The monkeys were jumping up and down laughing at the stupid human that was crazy enough to enter their territory. Mile after mile Tomba would pass the exhausted fellows along the way and he watched closely to avoid the dangerous traps. Tomba's father told him of the trees with no leaves that had the nooses of rope that would come down to catch the animals. It was necessary to have traps to keep the lions from the village, but now it only made it harder to complete the journey. Fortunately Tomba knew what to watch out for and kept his eyes open. Too bad all the young men didn't pay attention too busy trying to get to their quest Tomba thought as he observed his friend Obadele caught hanging upside down with a noose around his foot hanging from one of the trees.

Obadele was Tomba's friend a skinny blue black man, that from when they were very young, they grew up getting trained together. Obadele was the same age as Tomba but was more of a jokester he wasn't as serious as Tomba often not paying attention to the training. So Tomba couldn't help to rub it in. *"How's it hanging Obadele?"* Tomba was laughing looking up at his friend hanging from the tree. *"Now you joke Tomba, please help me down, before I become roast dinner for the animals!"* Obadele pleaded. Tomba cut him down, laughing at his friend and how silly he looked. *"Thanks Tomba, I should of paid more attention to the signs, I will continue my journey and let you finish yours"* then he turned to leave. *"Wait Obadele it's not a rule that we can't continue our quest together."* Tomba said knowing that Obadele needed help to finish the journey and not only was Tomba his friend but he would one day be his Chief who had to look after his people. *"Come along Obadele let's go together."* Obadele was overjoyed, and relieved now with Tomba with him by his side.

The two young men walked a few miles and talked about their village and how happy everyone was there and how they looked forward to getting back home to their women and to start having families. *"Yes future Chief I think in my loins I can add at least ten more people to our village, or maybe fifteen."* Obadele said laughing. *"I look forward to holding my son in my hands, yes I hope to give Asante many babies, but wait!"* Tomba yelled smelling a strange scent. *"Do you smell it Obadele?"* Tomba asked *"No, what is it Tomba?"* Obadele asked nervously. *"Stay calm Obadele it's a lion nearby I can smell his scent, when I say go, you climb up that tree!"* Tomba said sensing the lion was getting close sneaking up to the young men ready to pounce. The men walked a few steps then Tomba yelled *"Climb Obadele!"* Then Tomba took off running while Obadele climbed the tree. The lion jumped out the bush and went after his prey running behind Tomba getting closer and closer. Tomba ran as fast as he could, but still could hear the lion getting closer, then Tomba saw what he was looking for. The big patch of leaves on the ground Tomba ran with the lion right up on him so close and as the lion was ready to chomp on Tomba, Tomba jumped over the patch of grass, and too bad for the lion he didn't and fell through to the ground in a deep hole. Tomba had got to the edge of the hole and was holding on trying to pull himself up, while the lion was below jumping up trying to grab a hold of Tomba's feet. Tomba was trying hard to pull himself out of the hole before the lion got a hold of him when he heard. *"How's it hanging Tomba?"* Obadele laughed as he reached down and grabbed his friends hand and pulled him out of the hole. *"Thanks Obadele I'm glad I remembered about the trap in the ground, or I would be this lion's dinner tonight!" "No Tomba I thank you now twice because I would have been his snack. I'm glad you listened to the elders about the traps, now what do we do about this lion Tomba?" "We must kill the beast before he kills one of us."* Tomba said then took his spear and waited for the lion to get into position, then Tomba threw the spear and it stuck the lion right in the side and took the beast down. Tomba knew what had to be done this animal had killed a lot of animals and villagers. It was the enemy and the elders taught the young men once observing your enemy never let them get a second chance at you.

After that ordeal the two fellows walked off and found a spot to turn in and made a cover and rubbed their bodies with dirt to throw off any scent just in case another lion came through while they were sleeping. The young men slept a few hours then they woke up and ate and then took off walking in the hot sun, sweating and tired from the heat until they got to the tall mountain. Both men looked up the mountain then at each other shaking their heads. *"Tomba when you are Chief you have to change these traditions, seems to me risking your life through these test just to be called men is silly, look at how many young men that don't make it."* Obadele said confused. *"Yes, but look at how proud the ones are that do make it, that's how we will be once we complete this journey, and beside that's just the way it is, it's tradition."* Tomba said but realized there was truth to what Obadele had said.

Then both men started climbing up the mountain, and there were many stops along the way where the men had to stop and rest tired from the climb and the hot sun. Tomba wondering now was this worth it, until he thought of Asante, that's what he needed to get his second wind. Tomba started climbing and singing as he climbed up the mountain, until he realized he had got to the top. Tomba stood there proud that he had made it this far, then he looked around and saw the flowers. The red flowers that only grew in this season only on top of this mountain and when he went toward the bush of flowers, his heart felt a twinge when he saw something else. It was a special stone that his father had and craved in it "my beloved son" when Tomba was born and now it was placed by the bush. And to see it, made Tomba happy that he knew his father knew he would make it and he would be first. Tomba took the stone and held it in his hands, then tears fell down out of his eyes with him thinking, this is why they do this, it's one thing to say you're a man, but to prove it was another. Tomba went over and picked his flower and kissed it and said *"Asante, this is for you my love."* Then he put the flower in his bag and waited for Obadele to make it to the top. *"Finally, Obadele I thought I was going to have to come get you."* Tomba laughed jokily. *"No, my friend this I had to do on my own, now let me get this flower for my mate and let's go home."* Obadele said ready to get off the mountain and go home to start their new life as men.

CHAPTER TWO

HELL ON WATER

The trip back was easier, the two talked about making changes and Tomba knew the first thing he was gonna do when he was Chief was make Obadele his top elder. Tomba saw his village growing even though their tribe was smaller than the others and so far no one worried about trouble, all the tribes got along staying in their own territory, just trying to live and survive. The two men talked about how everyone would be waiting for them to get back and the big celebration that would be set up for the returning men and the women that would be waiting for them. Tomba thought about how sweet Asante was and how long he waited for her and in only a short time he would see her and his family and how proud his father will be.

    The sun was shining as they entered the village, but it was empty, no people, no celebration it was the middle of the day surly someone would be outside. *"Something's wrong Tomba."* Obadele expressed. Tomba already knew something wasn't right so he ran straight for his hut with Obadele following behind. *"Tomba look at the ground!"* Obadele yelled when Tomba looked down he could see lots of fresh blood all splattered around. *"Oh no!"* Tomba yelled wondering was it a village war with all that blood around. When Tomba got to his hut he wasn't ready for the sight he saw. Tomba's mother was covered with blood. *"Mother what happen!"* Tomba yelled. *"It's not my blood, son they took him; they invaded us and killed a lot of the old warriors and took the young ones and the women and young girls. Oh, Tomba it was horrible!"* She said with pain. *"Mother who took our people!"* Tomba shouted. *"The white faces, they came in the village and raided it taking all the young ones leaving us old ones to grieve."* *"What about father?"* Tomba asked shaken. *"Tomba he and the others fought a good fight, but was no match against the strange weapons with the metal stones, our spears was no use. This is your father's blood son, he died in my arms. He told me to tell you to go get the other villagers from the other tribes and be prepared for the next time these white faces came back!"* Wesesa cried then tried to wipe all the tears from her eyes. Tomba was now holding her, trying to hold on himself, not believing this horrible thing could be possible. *"Son, he said don't come after them, stay back and build the village back up, be the new Chief and keep the village safe something he failed to do."* His mother said sadly. *"Where is he?"* Tomba asked crushed. *"At the ocean where the white face's have their big hut on water and where they took my son Aiyetore!"* Wesesa broke down. *"Mother no they got Aiyetore!"* *"Yes all the young men and women, son they also got Asante. Your father and the elders tried to get them back, but they couldn't, now our village has been killed!"* She screamed in pain. Tomba kissed his mother and turned around to leave. *"Tomba no where are you going!?"* Wesesa asked overwhelmed with grief. *"You said it mother, I am Chief now and I have to go save our people!"* *"No son they will kill you!"* *"If I don't go help my people and without Asante I might as well be dead."* Tomba said and left with Obadele following ready to risk his life to help his Chief.

The two men alone with only spears ran toward the water and almost fell apart as they saw how it had been a battle with all the dead warriors laid out on the ground blood flowing from their bodies. Tomba saw how the white face men had lots of young men and women from different tribes on the ground with their hands behind their backs with rope holding them together. Some of the white men were putting the villagers into the strange hut on the water. *"Tomba, look over there!"* Obadele yelled as he pointed at Tomba's father lying on the ground with Aiyetoro and Asante both tied up and crying over the body. Tomba could hear Aiyetoro his brother asking them why are they doing this horrible thing. Then the white face man yelled something in a language at Aiyetoro Tomba had never heard before. He yelled at Aiyetoro again then one man hit him with a small weapon in his face. *"No!"* Tomba yelled then ran out to save his brother, totally not thinking how he was out numbered, all he saw was hate, anger and right then he jumped on the man that hit his brother hitting the man hard on his face. Aiyetoro and Asante was shocked to see Tomba there and now the other white faces came running and jumped on Tomba hitting him hard in the head. That's when Obadele came out of the bushes to help Tomba by poking his spear into the back of the one white face that was holding Tomba down. Tomba watched how the man fell off of him and yelled in pain then a big huge white face man came over and took a small weapon and pointed it at Obadele and BLAM it was a big loud sound and Obadele fell to the ground with blood coming from his head. *"No!"* Tomba yelled as the white face said something he couldn't understand. "Let's kill this nerga too!" "No, stop Mr. Turner, if you kill all the cargo we won't have anything to sell!" The Captain West said who was a younger thin white man. "Okay Captain, but I think this one is going to be a problem." Turner said trying to hold back Tomba. "Their all going to be a problem if we don't hurry and get them locked up in the ship, let's go!" The Captain shouted. Tomba watched as they took him and everyone else but he couldn't look at Asante he was so ashamed and hurt of all that had happen and that he couldn't save his people. And the screams and cries of all the people being led, and pushed into this floating hut was heartbreaking. Tomba was led right pass his dead father and friend now all he could think of was trying to get away and back to that happy home he had but knowing nothing would ever be the same.

Tomba and the others were led into this dark place and layed down and locked up on these cots. The men were on one side and the women were on the other side. *"Tomba, this is Asante talk to me, tell me what is happening?"* Asante asked from the other side of the ship. *"I don't know these strange people and why their doing all these horrible things, but don't worry I'll get us back home."* Tomba said still not believing what was happening. Then he drifted into a heavy sleep and when he woke up he was hoping he was dreaming, but he wasn't he was still tied together with these metal pieces laying on his back in between two other victims. *"Asante, Aiyetoro, where are you this is Tomba." "I am over here my brother, I saw the white faces kill our father, they must die all of them!"* Aiyetoro yelled mortified. *"Aiyetoro first we all have to get out of here."* Tomba said. *"Tomba this hut is moving on the water, the white faces is taking us from our home. We will never go home again all we can do now is in the memories of all our dead love ones we have to kill all the white faces!"* Aiyetoro shouted. Tomba knew that the anger Aiyetoro was experiencing was from seeing their father killed, but he also knew he had to know it wasn't just bad for him and his brother but for Asante and all the other villagers. Tomba was a born leader and he had to get them all back home. *"Aiyetoro I know it is hard, but we have to keep our heads together so we can all get out of this trap."* Tomba said even though it was so hard for him also after the sight of his father and best friend lying on the ground dead. Then a few of the other villagers said they would follow Tomba and do whatever he said, so he could lead them all back home. Everyone was scared and heartbroken. Time went on as Tomba laid there, the darkness and the heat was unbearable, and there was no place to relieve yourself so you had to lay there and do it, so the smell was horrible. Then the white faces would bring their food that was so bad Tomba wouldn't serve it to his animals. More time passed and it was very quiet other than the sounds of soft crying because everyone had lost someone, a love one taken from their home by these dangerous, murderous people. The only one they could depend on now was Tomba to get them out.

Tomba was able to look around and he counted over a hundred men and women, he studied the white face's when they talked and so far he figured out they were called Negro's and they kept talking about the ship. *"Keep talking white face, the more you talk the more I learn, then we will leave this awful ship!"* Tomba said to himself. The white men would come down to leave the food, but the smell was getting so bad Tomba could see that they couldn't handle it anymore. So they brought the villagers up to the top, so they could wash down the smell of the cargo, while they made Tomba and a few others stay down in the dark pit to clean all the waste from the cots and the floor. Tomba thought what a horrible job, but he was glad to be able to move around. Then Tomba made his way to his brother. *"Aiyetoro soon I will learn the white mans ways then we can plan to escape out of this madness."* *"Escape to where my brother don't you realize we have been on the water a long time, we don't know where home is. The only thing I want now is revenge!"* *"Aiyetoro we have to keep our heads and not let our anger destroy our plan of getting everyone out."* Tomba said *"Okay brother, I will try, but I miss our mother and our father so much!"* Aiyetoro cried *"I do too, I do too."* Tomba said sadly.

Later the white men led Tomba and his brother and the other young men up to the top of the ship. *"Oh glorious, never was I so happy to feel the air on my face."* Tomba said to himself as the sun was bright and warm, but when they saw all that water and no land some of the men started to panic knowing the hole the white men had them in was going to be as bad as where they were taking them. Aiyetoro lost it, he ran over to one of the white men. *"Please, let us go, we mean you no harm, we just want to go home!"* Aiyetoro begged in his language pulling at the white mans arms. "Hey, this negro is trying to attack me!" The white man yelled thinking Aiyetoro was trying to hurt him, that's when the huge white man they called Turner took his weapon and hit Aiyetoro on the head again and again. The blood was coming out his head; Aiyetoro was struggling looking at Tomba who could only watch in horror, knowing that if he helped he would get the same or worse. Finally it was over Aiyetoro eyes still on Tomba, but there was no more life in him. Tomba shook in pain, wanting to yell out, and his heart just broke as the white men picked his brother up and tossed his body out in the water, like they were throwing out some waste. "What's going on here Turner?" The Captain asked. "The Negro attacked we had to put him down!" Turners said. "Turner if we lose another nigger it's coming out of your pay, now take them below!" The Captain shouted. The young men was led back down the hole Tomba now crying to himself as the other young men told the rest of the captives what had happen. *"Coward, you stood and watched them kill your brother!"* One villager said stabbing Tomba in the heart. *"Fool, if he would have jumped in he would also be dead in the water, I know my Chief, he stayed alive to help us!"* Asante said. Tomba was speechless too broken hearted that he fought lions that weren't as heartless as these creatures. The lions killed for food, these people killed with no feeling, they had no hearts or souls so there would be no reasoning. Tomba had to have a plan, people were counting on him.

Later that night, while most everyone was sleeping some of the white men came down, and started picking out the women. "Oh I like this one!" "I want this plumb one." They were saying then Tomba started shaking as Turner walked past him and walked toward Asante. "I'll take this one!" He said. Then a white man loosen the women from their chains while they were yelling trying to get away until one got slapped hard across the face. *"Stop fighting or you will end up in the water!"* One of the captives told them. So the women were marched upstairs, Asante looked at Tomba and the fear in her eyes cut him, that was enough Tomba kept pulling and tugging trying to get out. *"Stop struggling young Chief, save your strength you can't get out I have tried"* One of the African men said. *"Where are they taking the women?"* Another asked. *"Somewhere no good!"* Another replied. Asante was frighten as the white men brought her and the other young women up to the top of the ship, then into one of the rooms where there was more white men sitting around drinking. None of the women knew what was in store for them until the white men started grabbing at their bodies, and then they each were pushed into small rooms. Asante saw the cot and started crying knowing now what was happening. When Turner came in the room he had a sly grin on his face. "Girl, you got a job a head of you, the men need some belly warming on this long trip, but I go first. I know you don't understand what I'm saying, but you will know what I'm doing and if you fight me, you won't make the journey back to land." He laughed. Then he grabbed at Asante's fabric and pulled it off that covered her breast then he yanked her cloth that covered her treasure. Asante thought to her self her treasure was for Tomba and she had been saving it all this time for him, now this strange horrible man was coming after it. *"No, no please stop, don't do this!"* Asante cried. Turner didn't understand and didn't care what she was saying. Asante tried to get away but after getting punched in the face a few times and tasting her blood in her mouth, she knew she was no match as Turner took her treasure from her, it was so painful and it hurt bad physical but more emotional. Then after the forth man came in and evaded her Asante was numb, she couldn't believe what was happening. Then Asante's mind brought her back and she remembered how she watched Tomba leave for his journey to manhood and how she had fixed up their hut. Asante had fixed up a wonderful spot in their hut to give Tomba her treasure, but she didn't get a chance these vile men took it from her, she silently cried and wished for death for them and for her.

    Later after the white men were finished they were taking the women back to the hole. All the women once pure now violated and now marched back with their heads down ashamed all of them never to be the same. While they were walking back Asante so overwhelmed with shame ran toward the edge of the ship and tried to jump off. "Grab her and tie her up tight, she is going to bring a good price, plus we got a long trip home." The white man said as another pulled her back. When the women was brought back down into the hole then locked up the men started asking questions. None of the women wanted to talk all ashamed hoping no one would find out. *"Asante, talk to me this is Tomba, are you well, did you see away we could escape this place?"* Asante took awhile before she spoke. *"Tomba I am no longer pure, they took from me what I was saving for you, our future is over all we can look forward to is death."* She cried. *"No!"* Tomba yelled that was all he could take these devils killed his father, brother and his friends, and took him from his mother and now took his woman who he waited for all his life. Tomba no longer thought about escaping all he wanted to do is kill the white faces. The rest of the ride Tomba was silent, he couldn't look or talk to Asante thinking how he had failed her and didn't protect her from these animals. Asante knew it would never be a mating with Tomba she would never be the Chief's woman or have his babies, now she was just a tool for the white men. Through this long journey on the ship a few times the young men and women would be taken up to be washed off and later the women would be taken up to relieve the white men and they would come back beaten shaking and abused. Asante and Tomba could no longer look at each other from the shame they were both feeling. There was times Tomba often laid on the cot wishing for death. The captives had given up hope in Tomba he was a beaten man. Everyone knew they had to go along with the white men, so they could stay alive. More time pasted and finally they had got to land, now the Africans was looking at this strange land and all these people wondering and frighten what was going to happen next.

CHAPTER THREE

THE BIG HOUSE

Tomba was a beaten man standing there with the other captives in a bunch all with their hands tied up, and Tomba wanting to hurt all the white men, now looking at a strange land full of them. Tomba saw no hope still wondering why these white men killed his family and brought him here. As the white men led all the captives off the ship, they took them to an area where all the white people men and women and children was all around staring at the Africans. Then Tomba heard the Captain talking to another white man who had on a strange garment covering his whole body.

"We lost twenty five cargos due to sickness on our journey back." The Captain said to Mr. Brooks a stubby middle age man who was the riches man in the county of Mississippi. Then there were other tribe men with these white people, Tomba thought maybe the new tribe men could help them get away but by the look on their faces of pure sadness and how they wouldn't even look up, Tomba figured they were just as bad off as him. Captain West on the other hand was glad this mission was over and told this old white man to start the bidding. The white man, people called Mr. Roads was the man working for Mr. Brooks who was over the auction. One after another a captive would be walked up to a platform then sold to the highest bidder. White people came around from all over, all needing slaves to pick their cotton, cook, clean and produce more slaves. Tomba watched and picked up and now knew they were called slaves and how the white people would yell back and forth while staring at the slave of their choice, then the slave would leave with them. Tomba saw how the white people would get more excited when the women were tooken up front. Tomba realized that they were getting chosen then going to their new home. When they got to Asante it was a lot of men yelling. The bidding started off high because Asante was a beautiful black young woman, who would be able to do a lot of work and give a lot of pleasure. Asante stood up front on the platform and finally looked at Tomba with sad eyes that had tears coming from them and wondering what was going on while Tomba looked up at her, all tied up unable to do anything, but shed tears with her. There were two men that had kept bidding back and forth until finally one of the owners gave a final bid, which shut down the other bidder, and he was smiling thinking he had won, until another bidder yelled fifty dollars over his bid. Tomba looked in horror as the auctioneer pointed and said "Sold to Mr. Turner, yes Turner had spent all his money on this journey to buy Asante. Turner smiled at Tomba in a sinister grin as he took Asante out of his life forever. After selling what he didn't need Mr. Brooks took the rest of the slaves for his plantation, Tomba was one of them.

Years had past Tomba was learning the ways of the white man. He learned their language and was taught how to work the fields from sun up to sun down. Tomba picked cotton, and then the slaves were given off one day to rest, only so they wouldn't fall off dead from being over worked. Tomba had met other black slaves that were born in this land. Chuck a slave his age was twenty five years old, he was a brown skin tall man that worked the fields, who hated the white man as much as Tomba. Chuck had a younger sister Mary a golden brown girl who worked in the Master's house. Mary looked to one day being free and doing something with her life instead of working for Mr. Brooks who had a wife named Jennifer. Mrs. Brooks hated blacks and if she didn't need them to clean she would never have them in her house. The Brooks had a Daughter Ronda who was eighteen years of age and like her mother hated blacks and got pleasure out of seeing the slaves suffer. Ronda would work them hard then she would get the Overseer Mr. Jones a stocky older white man to beat them. Mr. Jones got pleasure also beating the slaves, that was his job and he had been running the plantation for over twenty years. Then there was Lillie, Chuck and Mary's mother who was a big black sassy woman who cooked the food at the Master's house along with Mary and their father whose name was Rabbit, he was the head Negro for the slaves. Rabbit was the one the slaves went to with problems and he would either go to Mr. Jones or Mr. Brooks and they would come to him if they needed to ask about a certain slave. Rabbit got his name long time ago from the other white people, because he use to hop every time the Master called him.

When Tomba got to the plantation Rabbit worked with him and taught him how to stay alive but first thing he did was started calling Tomba, Tom. "Them white people don't like to hear those African names boy, you got to do what you have to, to survive." "But my name is Tomba, my father named me, why do I have to change?" Tomba asked "Because they won't be calling you nothing because you will be dead if you don't go along, do you think I care if they call me Rabbit, no at least I am here to hear it." Tom started to go along with what was expected and that was to wake up in the morning and pick cotton. Then the slaves would be taken back to their shacks to eat, sleep then wake up in the morning and do the same thing. On their day off the slaves would all get together and sing and dance and mate.

"What do we have to sing about, we are just tools to the white man!" Tom said frustrated at the slave's display of joy to Chuck and Mary one day observing the sight. "Tom, this is the only day of the week we get to be happy, why do you ruin it with your African talk, you have been doing this for years now!" Mary asked upset. "Because as an African we had more than one day to be happy, everyday was happy. We had our own land, our own huts, we loved and mated when we wanted to, we wasn't slaves, we were men and women just like the white people. We did our own work, raised our own children and we didn't whip and kill so merciless, we had real joy, this is not it!" Tom said upset. "Yes, but where is Africa, we don't know how to get there, you don't even know if your village is still there after the white man came and destroyed it, but I like you Tom would love to have my own fields to work and have my own family. I am so sick of picking the white mans cotton and making him rich!" Chuck said angrily. "Don't talk like that boy those words could get all of us whipped or killed!" Rabbit said walking by with Lillie and hearing the conversation. "No Rabbit it is my fault I was telling Chuck and Mary of my home." Tom said. "Well if you want to continue to live in our place, you got to stop that talk Tom, we all are here to stay, and it's not that bad." "Father you have been on this plantation so long that you don't see that you're a man like Master Brooks and why should you have to work for him. Why can't you have your own life, and what of me and Mary is this what you want for us the rest of our lives to be slaves to the white people?" Chuck asked. "Yes son because that's the only way you will stay alive!" Rabbit responded sadly then walked away. "Don't be so hard on your father Chuck at least we are living better then most of the slaves, we have the biggest shack and...." Lillie said but then got cut off by Chuck who said. "Yes and you bring us all the scraps from the Master's table." "Son we have a decent Master and when the time is right he will give you a woman to share your life with." Lillie said. "Mother all the women fit for me have been touched by the white mans tools, and the only reason why Mary has not been touched is because of you and father." Chuck said. "And we want to keep it that way so hush up boy!" Lillie said angrily. Chuck apologized to his mother, he respected and loved both his parents, but he hated the white man and wanted more out of life.

Mary was eighteen and also wanted more out of life she would observe Mrs. Brooks and her friends and the elegant dresses and jewelry and the hairdos and all the fancy stuff. Mary saw how they would ride up in their fancy carriages and sit around and sip tea all day. Mary wanted that, instead of cleaning floors in her traditional old oversize cotton slave dress. Ronda the Brook's daughter hated Mary more than any other slave because Mary grew up in that house. From an early age Mary would come around the house helping her mother cook and clean the house. Mr. Brooks had got use to seeing her and she was off limits to the other white men that worked for him because of Johnny. Johnny was his son who was now nineteen and wanted to be a teacher so he used Mary as his student and secretly taught her to read and write. Who she later taught Chuck and Tom, but this was not accepted in this white world, and if it was known teacher and student would be in lot's of trouble, but more so for Mary so it was their little secret. The only thing by learning to read and write Mary's eyes was open to so many possibilities.

One night Mary saw Tom outside looking at the stars she walked toward him and asked. "Tell me more about your home?" Tom looked at this young girl who was turning into a beautiful woman and it made him think of Asante and how he missed her and the children he would have had by now after spending seven years in this land and now he felt his heart breaking all over again. "I am sorry, Tom I didn't mean to upset you the other day. You was brought here from your home and your family to work around all these strange people, I know it must be hard, I am sorry for what I said." Mary said. "No need Mary I have watched you grow up, and I know your heart and you didn't mean to hurt me, but I come from a land where everyone was free to come and go as we please. We worked for ourselves and for the village and my father was the Chief. He was a good and fair man who along with my brother and my friend that was killed by the white man. They took me away from my mother and took my woman from me and left me with an heart with the love gone but now full of hate and no future." Tom said sadly. "Tom, you have had it rough, but your family loved you, don't you think they would want you to move on and make the best of what you have?" Mary asked. Tom thought about it and said. "Mary you and your family are the only thing good about my life now, my life is back in Africa, but one day I will have my revenge on the white man, that's the only thing that keeps me going!" Tom said. Mary shook her head and walked back to her shack and along the way she saw Johnny sitting outside the big house.

"Mary, hello come walk with me to the pond." Johnny said who was young and blond haired and had lots of schooling he was handsome and educated and white. Mary liked Johnny, she had grown up with him and he was always nice to her unlike the rest of his family. The two use to play together when his mother wasn't looking, and unlike the slave boys, Johnny was clean and smelled good, smart and rich. Everything a woman would want, but he was white and she knew it wouldn't look right by having those feeling. "You know Johnny I can't go walking with you at night, I will get in trouble mainly from my father and your mother." "No one is around Mary and I want to go to the pond, and like you said it's night, everyone is in their homes or asleep, now let's go." Johnny said all cheerful, not a care in the world. Mary thought why should he care if they got caught together she would be the one to get whipped, not him. Mary reluctantly walked to the pond and sat down and the two talked and talked. Johnny told Mary of his plans of starting a school nearby the house where he could teach the young kids. Mary thought that was so wonderful of him and by sitting and talking to him all night she found herself falling for him, by the time she got back to the shack she was happy no one saw her sneak in because she didn't want anyone to know her secret visit with Johnny.

CHAPTER FOUR

THE HOUSE NIGGER

The next day Tom and Chuck went out to the fields, and Rabbit, Lillie and Mary went to the big house for their daily routine. On one of the few breaks the slaves were given to get water and rest, Chuck and Tom sat down and began to talk. "Tom, I can't do this anymore, I got to get out of here, I want to be free and go to Africa, let's go together!" Chuck said finally at his breaking point. "What about your father and mother and your sister, what of them?" Tom asked. "I love them, but their like the other slaves say, they're house niggers. They have been in the big house so long they forgot they were slaves, but one day they will be reminded." Chuck said frustrated, but before he could finish Chuck got hit with the whip by the Overseer. "Get back to work Negro's, you had your five minute water break!" He yelled. Chuck looked at him with anger and started to lunge after him when Tom grabbed him. "No Chuck I have seen too many of my people killed by the white man, no more!" Tom said then they both went back to work.

    At the big house Mary was cleaning the Master's bedroom thinking about how much trouble she could have got into if she had got caught with Johnny and telling herself to never let that happen again when Johnny entered the room. "There you are Mary I enjoyed our night together." Johnny said happily. Mary continued to work with her head down trying to avoid his eye contact. "Mary what's wrong?" "What's wrong is the way you look and talk to me, that could get me whipped." Mary said now looking in his eyes. Johnny grabbed her and told her;

he wouldn't allow anyone to hurt her. "We grew up together you are my friend and I like you." He said. "Stop that talk Johnny, I don't want any trouble we are different people!" Mary explained. "My mind says one thing sweet Mary but my heart says another." Johnny expressed looking in her eyes and melting her heart he then leaned down and kissed her lips. Mary tried to back away but he brought her back to him and Mary forgot they were different people, he was a man and she was a woman in love. Now both of them had forgot everything and found them selves lying on the Master's bed hugging and kissing when Mr. Brooks walked in, closing the door loud to alert them of his present. "Oh no!" Mary yelled then jumped up and ran out the room. "I am sorry father, I…" "No need to explain son, I knew one day you would need to get your release, that's why I saved Mary for you. I wouldn't let any of the other men touch her through the years, but don't let your mother know your relieving your self with that negro woman, she don't understand that the negro women isn't here just to clean floors." Mr. Brooks said and then with a sly grin he patted his son on the back like he was a proud father who just saw his son take his first step. Johnny knew by his father's comment he didn't and wouldn't understand his affection for Mary.

Mary went back to work and avoided Johnny and Mr. Brooks. Later Mrs. Brooks came into the kitchen and told Lillie and Mary she was having a party on Sunday the only day the slaves had to rest and she wanted them to work with the party. "Yes maim, we will be here." Lillie said. "I know you will or you will get whipped and tell Rabbit I want him here also and make sure you all wash up, I don't want you niggers stinking up my party." She said then walked out the kitchen. "Mother just because we are slaves and don't have those fancy clothes that don't mean we are dirt!" Mary said upset. Lillie walked over to Mary and slapped her hard across the face. "Child, don't talk like that, especially in their house, don't you know you could get us all killed or put out on the fields to pick cotton all day!" Mary apologized to her mother understanding that her mother often worried about her family, and if her father was put out on the field he would die like a lot of the old slaves.

Later that night Lillie, Rabbit and Mary had got back to the shack, shortly after them Chuck and Tom came in tired and frustrated. On Chuck's back you could see the fresh whip mark on his bare back. "What happen son!" Rabbit yelled looking at the wound. "Overseer hit me so I could hurry up and get back to work. I wanted to pull him off his horse and take that whip and beat him with it and see how he likes it!" Chuck yelled. "Son, all that would do is get you killed if you could just hold on son I will try to get you and Tom work at the big house, but they don't want no angry negro there so you have to be…" "A good little house nigger, father no I rather pick cotton till I die before I clean the Master's house!" Chuck yelled. "So is that it, both you and Tom want to die in the cotton fields? I don't want that for you two and it has benefits being a house nigger. I can get the Master to give you two women, I think that's what you need." Rabbit said. "Father we can't even choose our own woman!" Chuck shouted. "Thank you Rabbit, but the white man took my woman on that ship coming over here it will never be another love for me." Tom said sadly. Mary listened hurt, that Tom's only love was taken from him and wondering if Johnny would be the only man she would ever love but never have.

The rest of the week went by with Chuck and Tom in the fields plotting to run away while Mary did all she could to not get caught alone with Johnny again. Then the night before the party Johnny caught Mary alone. "Mary you can't keep avoiding me in this house I miss our talks." Johnny said cornering her in the parlor. "Please Johnny I have to set up for the party or I will get in trouble with your mother." Mary said nervously. "I am sorry Mary I don't want you in trouble, I just want to see you more, look I got you something" he said then handed Mary a box with a beautiful beige dress with pearls on it. "Oh no Johnny I can't take this, but it is beautiful." She said overwhelmed. "Then take it and wear it for the party." Mary thought about it and she couldn't resist being able to for once wear a beautiful gown. Johnny put the box down and left the room. Mary took the dress and held it up close to her and turned around in circles, and for that instance she forgot she was a slave.

That night of the party Lillie had supper for her family and was ready to go back to the big house and she was now waiting for Mary to come out of her room. "Now you don't even get this one day to rest, mother?" Chuck asked. "No, they're having a big party and we all got to go back up and help." She said. Lillie would be over the food, Mary along with the other slave girls would serve and Rabbit would take care of the guest carriages. Chuck then whispered to Tom this is the perfect day to run away while their having their party. "What of your family, are you going to say goodbye?" Tom asked. "No, you can see where their lives are it's at the big house, and if they find out they will try to talk me out of it and if they don't know they wont get in trouble." Chuck said sadly. "I will miss them." Tom said sadly. "Me too, but I can't wait to get to Africa and see everything you told me about it. I dream about it every night and think of it while I am out there picking that cotton." Chuck said excited. That's what Tom needed to get him to move on was to see Chuck excited, it gave Tom the will to forget about his revenge for now and plan to get home and see his mother. Tom hoped when he got home he would get the villages together as Chief and one day come back and kill all the slave owners or maybe take them back to his land and make them slaves. "Yes, I would like to see if the lions like white meat." Tom thought to himself deep in thought as Lillie and Rabbit came out dressed in their best slave clothes.

Then Mary came out of her room dressed in this beautiful dress, she looked strange to her family. "Where did you get that dress and I know you can't wear it to the party!" Lillie said shocked. "Yes child you will get all of us in a lot of trouble!" Rabbit said surprised. "No, Johnny gave me this dress and told me to wear it." Mary expressed smiling feeling like those white women she was so use to seeing. "Johnny, it's Mr. Brooks to you, know your place girl, you been up at the big house too long, always around that white boy, that's why you never talk to the other black men. They ask about you and try to call on you and you don't give them any time, sister remember you're still a slave and he is the Master he owns you!" Chuck yelled. "Chuck you talk about leaving everyday, don't you think I get tired of cleaning floors or being yelled at by that woman. I want to be able to wear these lovely dresses and be free to love who I choose and Johnny will help me!" Mary yelled back. "No daughter Master Brooks won't help you just like they never helped me and your mother, we have been good slaves for a long time and all we got is a better shack, more food and less beating. That is all we can hope for because we are still slaves and son, I never forgot that, but I got to be an old man by keeping my mouth shut and doing everything Master said because through my years I have seen a lot of slaves killed for little or no reason. You young one's will never know how it feels to have to whip a slave to death. The white man wouldn't do his own killing; they made me do this when I was younger. Slaves I knew and ate with and after years of living through this, the Master moved me up to help at the big house. So call me a house nigger son, I rather be that, then to ever have to hold a whip in my hand again." Rabbit said with tears falling down his face. Chuck went over and hugged his father understanding now how his father felt and wondering if this would be the last time. Chuck then went over to his mother and sister and held them then he watched them walk over to the big house.

Rabbit was outside while the guest was arriving he started putting their carriages and horses away while Lillie and Mary went straight to the kitchen. When the other slave girls saw Mary they shook their heads wondering what Mary was thinking about. It was bad enough they had to cook and clean the Master's house and then at night being taken out of their shack to go please the white Master and his white workers, here this young slave girl comes in looking like them. "Mary what is the matter with you, you don't want to bring attention to the white man, you must of never been yanked out your room and made to please those evil men, because if you did you would not try to be beautiful to them." One said. "But still that does not matter, as long as you have a body and you're a woman that is all they care. And once you get tooken and have their smelly white bodies over you, then they send you back to your man and he can't even look at you for the shame of a another man entering you and him unable to help you. Then you have to lie to your children why you have to leave at night while everyone is sleeping, then you will see Mary, then you will see." The young slave woman cried.

Lillie listened not saying anything, knowing how it went, herself being a young woman and having to please the white man. After years of being used Lillie grew numb to what she had to do and men like Rabbit knew that's what was expected out of their women, they didn't like it but after a while it was just another job like cleaning floors. The younger slaves like Chuck was having problems with this, that is why so many was getting whipped and killed and shipped off to other plantations. Lillie knew Mary was making a mistake but if Johnny gave her the dress to wear and if she didn't it might be worst for her. Mary ignored the other slave girls, she wasn't going to be a slave all her life and she felt good in the dress, but when she walked out of the kitchen to serve the food Mrs. Brooks, Ronda and the other white women was appalled in shock. "Who does that Negro think she is!" One lady yelled. Johnny who was there looked up to see Mary standing there in the dress looking beautiful Johnny smiled at the sight of her. Ronda observed her brother and was shocked. "Look at my brother's face no, he can't like that nigger, mother look at Johnny!" Mrs. Brooks was more in shock watching her son and how he had that look. "Don't worry mother I will handle this!" Ronda yelled then walked toward Mary and grabbed the tray of food and started spreading the food all over the dress. Mary stood there in horror. "Mary oh, too bad I messed up your beautiful dress, I guess your gonna have to take it off!" Ronda said and laughed. Mary then turned to leave. "No, take it off right here slave!" Ronda demanded. Mary looked at her with all the hate she had in her then looked over to Johnny who had his head down with Johnny's father and all the white people that was there, he couldn't go help her or he would be disowned by everyone. Mary's eyes starting to tear up, as she stood there in the middle of the room with all those white people looking at her. Then in the corner of her eye she saw the other slave girls and her mother at the kitchen door all sad for her, but knew they could not interfere or they would be next. "I said take off that dress, or I will have the Overseer whip it off of you!" Ronda demanded. Slowly and sadly Mary took off the dress now standing there with only her undergarments on while all the white people laughed out loud. "Now go back to your shack and come back and look like the slave you are!" Ronda yelled. Mary ran out the room and passed her mother and the other slaves girls back to her shack.

Meanwhile Tom and Chuck were all packed up to go when Mary came running in. "Mary what happen to you?" Chuck asked shocked. Mary ran to her room and came out in her slave dress, the worst one she had. "Sister what is wrong?" Chuck asked again. "You were right my brother those awful people showed me my place. I am a slave and always will be." She said sadly. "Mary, me and Tom is running away come with us." Chuck said excited. Mary looked at her brother and Tom and after tonight she so wanted to leave the plantation but, said no. "I would only slow you two down, and I can't leave mother and father alone here, but you go, both of you get out of this horrible place and be free!" She said with tears in her eyes. "Mary someway I will make a way to come back and get you and mother and father and bring everyone to freedom." Chuck said. "Don't worry about us you go now, I will tell mother and father later." She said then hugged her brother. Tom then went over and hugged Mary tight. "I will never forget you Mary and after I get back to Africa I will build my village back then I will come back to get you." Tom told her. Then the two men snuck out the shack pass the gate and being everyone was at the big house at the party it was easy to get through. Mr. Brooks and the Overseer didn't worry about any runaways because all of the slaves knew by past experience that they would get caught whipped and sold or killed. The Overseer bragged and often reminded the slaves that no slave had ever got away, so not many tried until tonight. Tom and Chuck ran through the night and the tall grass then they got to an area that looked like a jungle this was Tom's element, it wasn't Africa but Tom was able to move easy through the forest. Chuck followed with mixed emotions already he was missing his family but he was so looking forward to a new life. Chuck knew he would of died if he had stayed any longer on that plantation and he knew no one ever escaped the plantation and got away, that's why he never tried but with this African leading the way they had a good chance that he had to take.

CHAPTER FIVE

A CHANCE TO LIVE

Tom was feeling like he was back home and the other slaves had told him that the way to freedom was up north. All Tom knew is he had to get to the water and get passed it, that was the way to freedom. Tom also knew it would be a long journey both men brought sacks full of food and water. The problem was getting a ship to take them to Africa. The men knew their plan had some holes in it, but their main goal was to get away and now they were doing it, that night they had made a lot of distant.

    Later back at the plantation, the party continued Mary had came back humbled she began to serve the food and listen how the white women joked about her new outfit. "Now that's better slave how dare you come in thinking you was like us, and where did you get that dress anyway?" Mrs. Brooks asked. Mary just stood there and didn't want to say until she got slapped across the face hard. "Tell me nigger who gave you that dress or did you steal it?" Mrs. Brooks yelled. "No I did not steal it." Mary said but she wouldn't tell Mrs. Brooks who gave it to her, even though she was disappointed with Johnny, she wasn't going to get him in trouble, because often other than tonight he was her only white friend. Mrs. Brooks was getting more upset by the minute and being that she had been drinking throughout the whole party didn't help. "Okay let's see if I can whip the answer out of you, Overseer get your whip out!" Mrs. Brooks demanded. "Mother not tonight we are having a party." Johnny said hearing the conversation and worrying about Mary. "No you got to do it now mother, you can't let your friends think you can't handle your niggers!" Ronda yelled. Mr. Brooks who overheard what was going on had been drinking and having a good time, didn't want to interrupt the party with a whipping, but over the years Mr. Brooks learn to just let his wife have her way. Mr. Brooks didn't care he had fell out of love with her a long time ago and he had plenty of young negro slave women to please him and Mrs. Brooks knew it. That's one reason why she hated the black women so much, they were getting that love from her husband that she needed and when Mary walked in trying to entice her husband that was it. Mary was scared she had never been whipped now she was going to see how the other slaves felt. Mrs. Brooks was really drunk now and so upset at Mary's disrespect to her so she had the Overseer take Mary outside and invited all the guest to come out and see. Mrs. Brooks wanted to show them and the other slave girls who she knew one of them would be with her husband tonight that she was still in control. When everyone got outside Rabbit went to his wife and asked what was going on. "They're going to whip our child Rabbit!" Lillie cried she had worked all her life trying to make sure her children wouldn't be beat, by being the best Negro slave to her Master and Rabbit having held that whip so many years and watching the flesh peel off the slave's body tore him up so much he wouldn't even whip his children growing up. Now he realized now why they both had attitudes that were so stuck on changing their situation. They have not experience real pain. They really didn't know how hard it was for most of the slaves and he tried to save his children from the pain but now his daughter was going to experience some and he couldn't do anything but stand there and cry.

The Overseer had taken Mary outside to the middle of the plantation and stretched both her hands and tied them to two posts. All the slaves stopped their singing and dancing to see what was happening and saw Mary stung up. "That is just what that house nigger needs, now she will know she ain't no better than us." One slave said. "Stop she is a slave like us!" Another said. "I know but she don't know it but after she gets beat she will know." The other said. Johnny pleaded with his father to stop the whipping to no avail. One thing Mary was glad that her brother was gone because he wouldn't have let this go on. The Overseer would have had to kill Chuck to stop him from helping his sister. Mary closed her eyes and said a silent prayer. The Overseer took his whip and swung it BLAM. Lillie and Rabbit held each other and cried and prayed for the Overseer to stop. The first hit, tore off the back of Mary's dress, she hung there taking in the pain. It was the worst she had ever had, but she wasn't going to cry out and she wasn't going to tell Mrs. Brooks that Johnny had gave her the dress. Then the Overseer swung again, Pop this one dug deep in Mary's flesh, it hurt so bad she thought she was going to past out. Then Pop again this time Mary cried out in pain, then the Overseer swung again then "Pop." "Oh!" Mary yelled. That was enough Johnny ran toward the Overseer and stopped his hand as he was going to hit Mary again. "Stop I gave her the dress mother, now stop the beating!" Johnny screamed. Mrs. Brooks shook her head in disgust. "Cut her down Mr. Jones." Then she looked at her son and said. "You're just like your father!" Thinking how her husband and now her son wanted the Negro women. The Overseer cut Mary down then Rabbit and Lillie went over and took their daughter back to their shack. Later Lillie was taking care of the wounds that was deep and that was embedded in Mary's back. "Where is Chuck and Tom?" Rabbit asked seeing they were not in the shack. "They are gone father, they ran off." Mary said lying on her cot in pain. "What, they ran, when!" Rabbit asked scared for them. "Early tonight while the party was going on, they left and I hope they get away and never come back to this evil place!" Mary cried. "Oh my son, if they catch him, their gonna kill him, why did you let him go Mary?" Lillie asked upset. Mary turned around and looked at her mother and said. "There was no way I could stop my brother if I wanted to, and I didn't. Chuck could not go on like this, he has to be free." "But if they catch him he will be dead!" Rabbit said. "Yes, but he will be free." Mary responded.

At this time Tom and Chuck had gone a long distance. "Stop we must rest." Tom said. "No we have to keep going so they won't catch us!" Chuck said excited. "No, Chuck our bodies need rest, as much as our minds." Tom said sitting down on a patch of grass. "Chuck when I was younger and before I took my journey to manhood my father told me don't let your mind try to out run your legs it won't happen, we have to rest and think." "All I can think about is getting to a place where I can be free Tom. You took your journey to be a man back in your homeland. A slave will never be a man always a possession to be worked and beat their whole life!" Chuck said. The two slept for a short time then got up and continued their journey to freedom. That morning the Overseer came busting in Rabbit and Lillie's shack. "Where is Tom and Chuck they are not in the fields!" "Sorry Master I saw them here last night." Rabbit lied. "Well their not at the fields so I guess we got a couple of runaways and if I find out you and your family know about this your going to get the same punishment their going to get when I catch them, you hear me boy!" The Overseer yelled. "Oh I hear you masa, I hear you good!" Rabbit said but was thinking "run boys run fast and far." The Overseer got a couple of white men and a few hunting dogs and got on their horses and took after Tom and Chuck. The other slaves rallied around Lillie and Rabbit, usually not caring for them because they thought they considered them better, but now they were slaves who was worried about their family. "You know they ain't gonna get away, they never do, and when there is two that run away they always kill one to scare us not to run again." One slave said. "I know but now they got the African if they can get to the water they will make it." Another slave said.

Hours went by and Tom and Chuck had got tired and sat down to rest. "We are going to make it Tom, we are gonna be free. And the first thing I am going to do is kiss the ground then I am gonna find me a woman to kiss and mate with!" Chuck laughed. Tom was happy to see Chuck laugh, he and the other slaves didn't know that kind of happiness. Some grew up being a slave and dying a slave, never to walk free among the flowers and the grass without chains and whips then Tom heard a sound. "Chuck I heard the dogs!" Tom yelled. "I don't hear anything Tom are you sure?" Chuck asked. "Yes I had to learn to listen for the lions so they wouldn't creep up on us and attack, it is the dogs. I can hear them and they are not that far." "No Tom I can't go back they will have to kill me!" Chuck yelled. Tom thought about what he was going to do and knew it was the right decision. "Chuck go, run through the water that will take off your scent I will lead the dogs a different way." "No you will be captured!" Chuck shouted. "I know, but I once tasted freedom, you have not" Tom replied. "But they will kill you!" Chuck yelled. "Chuck my life was gone long time ago, I just been waiting for my time for revenge, you getting away will be the start, go now!" Tom said. Chuck looked at Tom then hugged him. "Tell my family I love them." Then Chuck ran for the water. Tom ran toward the sound of the dogs and waited for them to get close. When one finally got sight of Tom he yelled and ran the opposite way taking them away from the water. The dogs were running after Tom who used his knowledge of the jungle and got a long way before the dogs caught up to him. Tom hearing the dog's right behind him ran toward a large tree and started climbing. Tom climbed that tree fast and far up and now was looking down at the barking dogs. It was a while before the Overseer and the other white men caught up to the dogs and Tom. "Come down nigger or I am gonna shoot you!" The Overseer yelled and pointed his gun at Tom who didn't move until the Overseer shot into the trees close to him shooting off a limb on the tree. Tom slowly crawled down as the white men pulled the barking dogs back. "Where's the other one, where's Chuck!" The Overseer yelled. Tom let the Overseer hit him a few times before he pointed in the opposite way of Chuck and told him that Chuck had ran that way. So the Overseer tied a rope on Tom's hands and pulled him and they all went to look for Chuck. Finally after a while they figured out Chuck was gone and the dogs had lost the scent. "You know nigger if I didn't have to bring one of you back you would be dead, but when I get you back you will wish you was!" The Overseer yelled and was shock to see a smile on Tom's face. Chuck is free that's all Tom was thinking about.

Back at the plantation Mary was laying on her cot in pain while Rabbit and Lillie had went back to work back at the big house when she got a visitor. "Mary!" Johnny yelled in shock seeing her lying on her stomach in all those bruises on her back. Mary looked up to see Johnny and saw the sympathy in his face, he truly was sorry for what happen but it was too late. "You should not be here Johnny you're going to get me beat again!" Mary said upset. "I am sorry Mary I never meant for this to happen, I can't understand how people can do other people like this." He said sadly. "Because you, your kind, are people we are slaves Johnny we don't count." Mary said. "What a world we live in that treats people like this!" Johnny said now upset. "Then change it, you can do it and I thank you for stopping the Overseer last night. I knew I should not have worn that dress, I just wanted to be beautiful." Mary cried. "You are and I will never let that happen to you again, now I must go." Johnny said then walked out.

That night the Overseer got back dragging Tom through the ground. The Master had everyone come out of their shacks to see what happens when you try to run away. The Overseer tied Tom up to the posts to be beat, Tom had his head down he was already worn out by being drug so long. When the slaves came out of their huts all of them wondered where Chuck was. "Rabbit where is our son?" Lillie asked. "Lillie they only let one live, so he must be dead." Rabbit cried. Lillie broke down then ran in the shack and told Mary. Rabbit listen to his family crying in pain and his thoughts of his son, now gone, if it was not for his wife and daughter he would of went over and strangled the Overseer's neck.

"Okay, boy let's put on a good show!" The Overseer laughed as he held up the whip to beat the African. Tom looked up at him thinking my body is an empty shell; your people have already hurt me when you killed my father and my brother and my friend. You hurt my woman and took what was mine, you took away my mother, that is pain, that whip can't hurt me. The Overseer began to hit Tom with the whip and with every swap you could see the white people smile and you could hear the slaves moan, but nothing from Tom. Tom took every blow without a word. The Overseer was getting angry and screaming "Yell nigger!" between every swap finally after getting tired the Overseer stopped and yelled "Cut this slave down he must be dead!" Rabbit and the other slaves ran toward Tom and cut him down and carried him to the shack. Mary and Lillie both in tears as they laid Tom down then his eyes slowly opened. "You're alive!" Another slave yelled. "Thank you God!" Lillie yelled then started taking care of his wounds. Rabbit sat down next to Tom. "Tom tell me did my son have a quick death or did they make him suffer?" Rabbit had to know and now with more slaves coming in all waiting to hear. Tom looked up and smiled and said. "CHUCK IS FREE!" The shack erupted in screams and tears of joy. The family all hugged each other Mary smiled at Tom and said. "Thank you!" The cheers were so loud Mr. Brooks could hear it at the big house. "What's wrong with these slaves!" He asked. Then the Overseer told him how Chuck had got away. "Mr. Jones let's not let this happen again, I can't afford losing anymore slaves so let's make an example out of Tom!" Mr. Brooks shouted.

CHAPTER SIX

TO LIVE AND NOT LOVE IS DEATH

Fifteen years had passed Tom was now forty years of age and still a slave, Johnny was sent away to another state for schooling Mrs. Brooks wanted him away from Mary. And after Johnny left the Master made his move and took Mary one night while his wife and daughter was away. Mary now understood why the other slave girls felt the way they did, it was the worst experience of her life, it was worst then getting whipped but the Master enjoyed her young body and took her often. Rabbit and Lillie tried to ease her pain knowing this is what happens to black slave women. Lillie and Rabbit was still working at the big house and Tom was still in the fields but one of his punishments for running away was he was not allowed to have a woman. The Master thought that was worse than getting whipped to not be able to be with a woman, but for Tom after he lost Asante his heart was close. Until Melissa and her family was bought and brought to the plantation.

Melissa was a dark skin young woman with curly hair and brown eyes and big hips. When Tom saw her she was the first woman in a long time to open up his emotion. Tom found himself thinking about her often. Melissa and her parents were all put out in the fields to pick the cotton and Tom heard the Overseer saying that Master Brooks won these slaves in a card game with another slave owner. Tom was very upset how these slave owners could wager peoples lives in a simple card game. Tom wanted to yank the Overseer off his horse and start choking him, then he smiled when he thought of Chuck and wondered how he was. "What are you so happy about Tom, do you enjoy picking cotton?" Melissa asked. Tom was startled to see her and to hear her talking to him. "No I don't enjoy picking cotton, I am use to it. I was just thinking of something pleasant." "What is pleasant about how we live Tom my family and I have worked our whole lives taking care of white people. I am now thirty three years of age and so far no mate or children, always being shipped off to plantation to plantation and seeing so many slaves whipped and killed, I know of nothing pleasant." she said sadly. "One day Melissa, I will tell you of my land and all the freedom and joy we had." "You were free Tom, you must tell me how it feels!" Melissa said and her eyes lit up like big diamonds and it did something to Tom's heart. "Later, now we have to get back to work before the Overseer gets out his whip."

That night at the shack Tom was all smiles, Mary and Lillie was watching him, then Lillie asked Rabbit. "What happen to Tom, look at his face he's smiling?" Lillie asked surprised. "Tom, what are you so happy about son?" Rabbit asked. Tom looked at his new family and how happy they were for him, because he was family to them. "Rabbit, I need for you to ask the Master if I could have a mate." "What, who!" Mary and Lillie asked surprised. "The young woman Melissa has made me want to have a family like yours." Tom said. "It is about time Tom, the white man took a lot from us, but they can't take that feeling of mating with a good woman and having children." Rabbit said looking at his family. "What about you Mary lot's of young men want to spend time with you, don't you think it is time daughter?" Rabbit asked. Mary lowered her head, after having to satisfy the Master so long she didn't know if she could mate with a man without thinking about how her body is not really her own, but she decided to try. "Ask for me also father." She said. Lillie was overwhelmed with happiness. "I will ask him." He said happily.

The next day Rabbit went into the big house and saw Mr. Brooks sitting in his chair smoking his tobacco. "Masa sir can I have a word with you?" Rabbit asked with his head down making sure he didn't look the Master in the eye. "What is it Rabbit, I am very busy!" He yelled. "I know Masa I am sorry to bother you but it is for my children. Tom and Mary they are well above mating age and I was wondering if you could allow them to mate and have children. I know you were upset at Tom for trying to run away, but that was a longtime ago and he is a strong African he could bring a lot of strong boys to help work the fields because most of the slaves are getting mighty old sir." Rabbit explained. Mr. Brooks thought about it and it was true they needed more workers and the price for slaves was high Tom could bring forth a lot of slaves. "Okay, Rabbit, Tom can have a mate, but Mary can not!" "Why Masa!" Rabbit asked shocked. "Because I said so, now get out!" Mr. Brooks yelled he wanted to save Mary for himself. Mary belong to him and she was his favorite, he thought about his son Johnny and how he had saved her for him all that time, but now that Johnny was gone, why waste a good piece of flesh. Rabbit walked out so upset and angry at how the Master would not allow his daughter to have a man. Mr. Brooks had went through all the young black slave women on the plantation, but he chose Mary to keep to himself. Rabbit didn't know that Mr. Brooks didn't touch Mary before because he was saving her for Johnny, but after Johnny left for school he couldn't wait to invade her.

Later back at the shack "Master said Tom you can have a woman, but Mary…" Rabbit stopped and put his head down shamed and said. "Mary he said you could not." "I wish I would of ran off with Chuck!" Mary said upset. "I wish none of us had to live like this, I wish we all could be free." Lillie said sadly. The family ate in silence everyone having their own thoughts and sad for Mary's fate. Mr. Brooks was going to use her until she was too old then he was going to put her out in the fields like he did all the others. Tom was sad for Mary and was feeling now that to live and not love is death, so the next day when he saw Melissa in the fields he made his move. "Melissa, when we have our next day of rest I would like to tell you more about my land and about the sweet taste of freedom." Tom said feeling like a different man, not a slave but a man with hope.

So when the day of rest came, Tom put on his best slave clothes and nervously went to the outside area where all the slaves got together to sing and dance. "Look Lillie its Tom!" Rabbit said surprised to see him because this was the first time he came to a gathering. Usually he would say he didn't have anything to sing and dance about, but most of the slaves looked forward to this day where they could all be together, without the whips and the cotton and the Overseer. Tom walked over to Lillie and Rabbit and watched the slaves dancing and singing and it took him back to Africa and how the village people would also celebrate life. "Where is Mary?" Tom asked. "The Master called her to the out house." Lillie said sadly. To the slaves the out house was a small place outside the big house where the Master and the other White men took the women slaves. "How can you say that with out anger doesn't it make you want to hurt the white man!" Tom said upset. "Every time son, but would that stop the next one, no then it would surly cost our life, and what can you do dead, nothing. So you realize that it is like a house you let a stranger in (the white man) but you don't like it and when they leave your glad they left. Then you have a friend (the slave man) and when he comes in your happy their there and you don't want them to leave." "Back in Africa where I come from we don't let strangers in our hut!" Tom said. "That is where you come from, but here we don't have a choice the stranger owns the house and he can say who can come and go in the house, he can even stop the friend from coming in, you understand." Rabbit said. "No, Rabbit I will never understand how they can take our women, why don't they mate with their own?" Tom asked "Because the white men like taking, and they know their women want to give it freely, but NO they have to take it from the young slave women. Then they give them children then ship the children off to other plantations because the white women don't want to see their husbands offspring walking around." Lillie said sadly having two children herself shipped off and thanking God so far the Master's seed hadn't landed in Mary.

Tom thought about Mary and hoped one day she would be free of the Master's vile touch, but after the escape the Master made sure it was always someone on watch at the gate. Tom thought maybe if he tried he could get pass, but he was a little older then the last time, but he still looked forward to be free, but now he wanted the touch of a woman and the woman he wanted was Melissa who was standing there among all the other slaves smiling happily. Melissa's beautiful black face and sparkling eyes and her white teeth she would show when she smiled and her body that was so curvy and her breast that her garment could hardly contain. Tom felt his manhood awaken, the way it did before with Asante and just the thought of her made Tom's heart break, wondering what kind of life she was having. Was she in the fields or the big house, was she allowed to mate with another slave or was she like Mary the Master's chosen one. And now with Mary like a sister to him all Tom could think of was killing the Master and hoped and prayed that Melissa's beauty would be over looked and she would stay untouched. "Tom there you are, I looked around for you, now you must tell me about this Africa!" Melissa said all excited. Tom smiled, most slaves did not want to hear about freedom when they could not have it, so for years Tom stopped talking about it.

"I come from a land where the people are free to live and love as they please, you can come and go where ever you wanted. The people lived in harmony, helping each other when needed for the sake of the village. No whips and chains no working from sun up to sun down, no slave owners or Overseer's to keep us down. My people were proud men and women who had our own huts and families. My father was the Chief who was a good and fair man that took care of his people as much as he could until..." Tom said then stopped just thinking about his father brought tears to his eyes. "Tom I can't imagine freedom and it is hard to miss what you never had so we make the most of what we have and nights like this is special for us slaves, because it is maybe close to freedom as we can have, but one day I hope and pray to be able to be free and love, but for now I can't be free, but I do have and want love." Melissa said looking into Tom's eyes. Tom was tooken back looking back in her eyes and knowing now she felt like he did. The two talked till it was time for all the slaves to go back to their shacks.

The next day Tom went back to the fields with a different outlook. "Mr. Brooks that African, he is working like three slaves into one, because he is fancy for that new slave you bought, but I thought we wasn't going to let him have a woman, that was his punishment." The Overseer said. "But like you said Mr. Jones, he is working like three slaves, that is more profit and we hope he can produce more African slaves, we need them." Mr. Brooks said. The Overseer walked off upset thinking "We could have a lot more workers if the Master would stop pregnating the young slave women then shipping the off spring away" but he was the owner and what he says goes. But Tom had embarrassed him by helping Chuck get away, so he was going to get even. "That's okay African I am not done with you!" He said slyly.

Weeks went by Tom and Melissa would be together as much as they could. "Rabbit could you ask the Master if I could have one of the empty shacks?" Tom asked. "It should be okay, with so many of the old slaves dying there is a lot of empty ones, why or you ready to jump the broom?" He asked happily. "Yes, Rabbit I am ready, I just hope Melissa will want to jump this broom with me." "Why wouldn't she, you're a good man, I hope for much happiness for you Tom." Mary said happy and a little jealous that she couldn't have the same thing. "I want to thank you family for taking me in and making me a part of you." Tom said humbled. "Boy, I can't explain how happy I am that you helped my son get away and I am praying he has the freedom we all want." Rabbit said. "Yes Tom we love you, but it is time for you to start a family so go get her!" Lillie said tears flowing down her eyes. Tom hugged his family then went to start a new one.

When Tom got to Melissa's shack it was dark and everyone was asleep. Tom had to sneak to not wake the watcher, the white men who watched the plantation. Tom went around to the side of the shack and knocked lightly. Melissa heard the knock and got up and went outside to see Tom standing there. "Tom what are you doing here you will get us both whipped." Melissa said surprised. "I am sorry Melissa but I could not wait till morning. I need for you to be my woman, please be my mate." He asked nervously. Melissa smiled. "I would love to be your mate, but I have to tell you, I am not pure." She said sadly. Tom was old enough and figured a beauty like Melissa had not went by untouched. "To me you are pure, and I look forward to mating with you and hopefully having many children." He said.

"Tom that is not all, once when I was a young girl, I was in love with Joshua a young slave boy. We both loved each other and was allowed to marry, and everything was fine and we had a son." Melissa said tears now flowing from her eyes. "The owner was a decent Master but then he died and we, my man and my child and father and mother were sold to these evil people. Our new owner and his men had an appetite for us young slave girls. The first time I was tooken, I wanted to die but I still had a man and a child and my father and mother to live for, but my man was having a hard time. Every time they called for me at night he would get mad and madder, then one day the owner sold my son. When they put my son in the carriage we cried so hard and my heart felt like it broke into a million pieces. My man went wild he attacked the owner and was shot down right in front of me and for so long I never thought of happiness again until I saw your face, that is my story Tom." Melissa said then lowered her head in shame. Tom lifted her chin to look in her eyes. "I don't believe any slave has not went through pain by the white man. I loss my whole family by their hands but now my love I want to start a new one, let's not let them take this love from us." Tom said and hugged her as she wept for joy. The marriage was set up and planned for the next rest time. All the slaves were excited there were only a few good times on this plantation this would be one. Melissa and Tom were so excited. "Tom I have our new shack ready for us after we get married." Melissa said happily. That brought back memories of Asante and how she had done the same thing by getting their hut ready, but the white men destroyed it. "Nothing will stop this one!" Tom thought to himself and could not wait to mate with Melissa, since having missed out first waiting for Asante to share his love with her. Then after they took her from him he had no desire for another love, and then later being denied a woman. Now he was ready and for once in a long time he was happy.

Melissa went back to her shack with her family beaming; it made her heart happy to see Tom happy. Lot's of slaves told her of how Tom was the unhappiest slave on the plantation. Melissa helped her mother clean the shack while her father was already asleep being old and had worked in the fields all day when the Overseer came busting in their shack. "Girl let's go!" He yelled. "Overseer Sir, my work is done for today." Melissa cried. "That was today I got work for you tonight!" "Please Master I am to be wed tomorrow." Melissa cried. "Fine get married tomorrow, but tonight you take care of me, let's go, don't let me have to tell you again or you gonna have some fresh whip marks to show Tom!" The Overseer yelled. Melissa had no choice and her mother told her to go before he hurt her. When the Overseer got to the outhouse with Melissa he pushed her in and told her. "Tell Tom this is my gift to him!" Then he laughed out loud, while he laid his big smelly body on top of her and took her. Melissa closed her eyes and thought of Africa and being free then it was over and he let her go. Melissa slowly walked back to her shack, her mother was waiting for her. "It is okay girl I know how you feel" seeing the pain in her daughters face. "Mother I have to tell Tom." "No you don't what will it do but upset him to where he might strike back and get hurt and rob from both of you happiness. No girl you marry the African and you have many babies and then they will have babies until one day one of them will be free and our blood will run in their veins and we will be free!" She said with tears in her eyes. Melissa and her mother held each other and prayed for that day.

The next day Melissa was hurting but when she saw Tom and how happy he was her heart mended. The women slaves had fixed up the gathering spot and had one of the old slaves men say a few words then Tom and Melissa jumped over the broom and became one. All the slaves was happy dancing and singing, then Tom showed the slaves an African dance and Melissa told him to tell them about his land. Most of them listened with awe about a land where they could be free to do their own will, but some were upset. "Don't talk of such things we will all get whipped!" One slave said. "No I want to hear more about freedom." Another said. Then Tom told them of a dream he had. "Here in this land they have a white man that controls everything, they call him The President, back in my land my father was the Chief and one night I fell asleep and woke up and it was a different world where we was free. Where we were equal, we had our own land and nice huts and Mary our women were able to wear beautiful dresses. We didn't have to worry about the white man coming in the middle of the night taking our women and we had a black Chief, a black President." Tom said. All the slaves sat there in shock with their mouths open until one old slave said. "African you are crazy, this is the white mans land what your saying will never happen!" He said angrily. "Well Tom I like your dream and that is one thing they can't take from us." Melissa said and then took her man's hand and led him to their new home. That night Tom finally experienced the woman's touch, it was over twenty years later and for Tom that was what he needed to make him want to continue to seek freedom, he wanted more for his woman. As time went on the cotton fields didn't seem to bother Tom as much because his nights with Melissa were wonderful. The Master had told the Overseer and the other white workers that Melissa was to have strong African slave babies. The Overseer didn't like that because he wanted to get back at Tom and he knew that would do it.

CHAPTER SEVEN

A GHOST FROM THE PAST

Life was going somewhat the same back at the big house. Lillie and Mary still working there with no problems until one of the white men told Ronda that Mary was her father's favorite belly warmer and they were often at the out house. Ronda couldn't wait to tell her mother who still hated Mary from that night when she came in wearing that dress and she found out it was from her son. Mrs. Brooks wanted to sell Mary but Mr. Brooks wouldn't let her telling her she needed to stay with her family. "No you wanted that slave for you husband!" She said to her self so she had to plan everything just right. First she wrote to Johnny and told him to come back home she was really ill, she lied and a week later Johnny had came back home.

Mr. Brooks was startled to see his son, but Johnny's mother knew what she was doing. After Johnny talked to his family he went to look for Mary. Mary was cleaning the kitchen thinking about freedom when Johnny waked in the kitchen. Mary saw him and dropped the dishes she was holding on to the floor breaking all of them. Johnny had grew to be a handsome man, tall with his blond hair and blue eyes, he was dressed up in a nice suit and smelling like fresh air instead of dirt and sweat like the young slave men. "Mary how have you been, I have to tell you all about my trip up north. I have learned a lot and now I am a teacher!" Johnny said excited. Mary stood there listening and shocked to see him and wondering how he could think things was still the same, wondering if he knew how his father had been invading her regularly.

"And Mary guest who I saw you will never believe it, I was so surprised it was Chuck!" "Chuck! You saw my brother, where is he, how is he!" Mary asked excited. "He is well; he is free and has a wife and three small children. He told me when I ever got back home to make sure that his family knew he was well and one day he hoped you all could be together." Mary cried tears of joy. "Johnny you know you must not talk of this, if your father..." "Don't worry yourself Mary." Johnny said cutting her off. "I will never tell my father about this and back where I was there is places where the black people are free!" He said. "Please Johnny tell me more!" Mary said excited and happy to be taken away from her slave life. The two talked and laughed together like old times. Back in the dinning room Mr. Brooks had been sitting in his chair doing accounts and when he got done he went to look for Mary he was needing to relieve his self and when he heard laughing in the kitchen he walked in and saw his son Johnny and Mary and a twinge of Jealousy hit him. Mr. Brooks excused his self and walked out not wanting his son to know how he had been taking Mary's body often; he remembered how Johnny had strong feeling for this slave.

Later back at the families shack Mary told her parents and Tom and Melissa what Johnny told her about Chuck. There were tears and shouts of Joy and for Tom it was much more because he knew with his help Chuck was free. "I have another surprise I am with child." Melissa said excited. Tom beamed with pride and made a promise to himself that his family would be free also. Back at the big house after dinner Mr. and Mrs. Brooks and Ronda and Johnny all sat in the parlor talking Ronda and her mother smiled at each other watching Mr. Brooks squirming nervously. "What is the matter father are you ill, your sweating?" Johnny asked. "No I am fine and it is nice how you recovered from your illness Jennifer." Mr. Brooks said starting to realize what was going on. "It is nice that you notice husband, being that I don't see much of you." She said looking at him glaring back at her angrily. "Father do you have a new business that is keeping you busy?" Johnny asked. "I would not say business brother it is more like pleasure." Ronda said fueling the fire. "Shut up both of you, Johnny does not need to hear your nonsense!" Mr. Brooks shouted. "What Jack you ashamed to tell your son that you spend most of your time at the out house with that slave girl Mary!" Mrs. Brooks said shocking both men. "Well it is better than lying next to you Jennifer!" Mr. Brooks yelled then walked out the door. Shortly after Johnny was at Mary's shack, he knocked on the door; it was really late so everyone was sleeping. Johnny knocked again then Mary came to the door dressed. "What Mary did you think I was my Father?" Johnny asked upset. "So you know." She cried. "How long has this been going on?" He asked. "As soon as you left." Mary cried. "How could he, goodbye Mary!" Johnny said then walked off in disgust. Mary shook her head. "He acts like it is my fault." Mary said to herself then went back inside. When Johnny found his father he lunged at him "Why father, why Mary!" "Stop acting stupid she's just a slave. I saved her for you all those years and then when you left I took what is mine. I own her all of her, now if you want some, you can take her to the out house also, you own her too son." Mr. Brooks replied emotionless. "Father I don't believe in treating people that way. I live a different life and I am going back to it and I will never come back here." Johnny said disgusted and walked out and when Mrs. Brooks found out she was livid. "See what you did your running our son away all because of that nigger slave, you get her off our land now or I am leaving and I will make sure everyone knows you threw your family away for a slave!" She yelled.

Later Mary found Johnny in their special place outside sitting looking at the stars. "I was looking for you Johnny I am sorry I could not tell you what your father was doing to me I was ashamed." Mary said sadly with her head down ashamed. "Mary it is not your fault, but I won't stay here I am leaving in the morning and never coming back." Johnny replied disgusted. "Please Johnny take me with you, I want to be free!" Mary begged. Johnny looked at her with sadness. "Mary I am sorry, but I can't take you I have a wife and a child and we have a home back there where I am a teacher, but I care about you and I don't like what my father is doing to you." Johnny said sadly. "But you can't help me your just like the others, goodbye Johnny and have a happy life." Mary said and walked back to the shack.

Later back at the shack "Girl you did not think he would be different, their all alike, so come off the clouds and get use to this life." Rabbit said. "No father like Chuck one day I will be free!" Mary replied then there was a knock on the door it was a slave that was sent to get Mary to come see Mr. Brooks at the out house. Mary got up and left the shack, Rabbit was hurt knowing his daughter would not be the same after Johnny turned his back on her. "Now she knows." Rabbit said then went back to sleep. When Mary got to the out house she saw a carriage Mr. Brooks and the Overseer, who walked toward her and chained her hands then, pulled her to the back of the carriage and tied her in. Mary knew now they were sending her off the plantation but she wasn't going to give them the satisfaction of screaming. "I am going to miss you girl, but the wife says you have to go and I will just have to get me a new belly warmer." Mr. Brooks laughed with the Overseer laughing along with him. "Do you think this is punishment, I can't wait to get away from your pale smelly body." Mary said then she got slapped across the face by the Overseer. "I am going to make sure your new owners keep you out in the fields picking cotton." The Overseer said. "I look forward to it, it will be better than having another smelly disgusting white hand on me!" Mary replied then the Overseer took his stick and hit her repeatedly knocking her out then he drove her off in the night. Mr. Brooks then looked up at the big house and could see his wife and daughter Ronda smiling out the window.

The next morning Johnny left, and when Lillie and Rabbit found out that Mary was sold to another owner, both of them pleaded with the Master but was told that if they did not want to be put out on the fields they had better go back to work. That night Tom was so angry he wanted to hurt everyone white. "No Tom you have a woman and a baby to come, don't lose that. We can only pray Mary was sent to a better place, but I will miss her so much!" Rabbit said then broke down. Lillie sat at the table numb. "After all the years we worked in the big house for that family, being called house niggers by our own kind. Some times even sticking up for that family and he has the nerve to tell me I better be glad that I get to stay in their house instead of picking cotton. Okay Master I will cook your food and I will make sure every dish of food that is on your table has my black spit in it!" Lillie said more upset than Tom has ever seen her.

The next few months went by quiet no slave wanted to dance or sing after the Master got rid of Mary. If it wasn't for Melissa and his child to come Tom would of surly hurt the Overseer. Melissa was later brought to the big house to replace Mary, then Rabbit got the Overseer to move Melissa's mother and father to the big house to help clean. That brought a little relief to Tom that Melissa and her family was not in the hot cotton fields anymore. Months later the night came when Melissa was to deliver the baby. Rabbit and Melissa's father and Tom waited nervously while Lillie and Melissa's mother helped to deliver the baby. Hours went by then Tom heard the sweet sound of a baby cry. Lillie came out the room looking sad. "It is a boy." She said to Tom. Tom jumped up and down. "I have a son, I have a son!" Tom yelled. Lillie looked at Rabbit and he knew by the look on her face twice he went through the same thing. When Tom entered the room Melissa and her mother was weeping while her mother held the baby. "May I see my son?" Tom asked Melissa's mother who then handed the baby to Tom and the baby was a pale white with no hair, then he opened his eyes and Tom saw the blue eyes. "No Melissa, No!" Tom yelled. "I am so sorry Tom it was only that one time the Overseer took me the night before we mated!" She cried. "It was not her fault Tom, you know how it is!" Melissa's mother tried to explain. Tom handed the baby back to her and walked out the room. Tom was in total shock, this was suppose to be his first child the tears fell off his face as he sat outside in the cold winter night. Rabbit walked over and sat down next to him.

"Don't give up Tom the next child will be yours, I have been through this also." "Rabbit you can not make this better, the Overseer did this to hurt me, so I am going to hurt him!" Tom said upset and then got up and ran all over looking for the Overseer until he found him in the out house with a young black slave girl that couldn't be over fourteen years of age. "Girl I am going to make you a woman tonight!" He said smiling to the young scared girl. Then she heard a loud sound then the Overseer with his pants down around his ankles fell over. Tom stood over him with a stick that had his blood and hair on it from the blow Tom gave him. "You won't be making any babies tonight, go back to your shack girl!" Tom said. The young slave girl got up and ran out relieved. Tom then took the stick and beat the Overseer till there was blood everywhere while yelling. "Scream white man, scream!" until the Overseer was unconscious. Tom looked down at him and said. "Now you feel the pain!" Then Tom left and started running, he got pass the gate unnoticed and he ran all night while the snow came down, until he finally had to stop. Tom found a patch of land and dug a hole and got in and covered it up with dirt then went to sleep and as he slept the snow came down then more ice came down and it mixed with the dirt and it packed the ground with Tom in it and he still slept until something magical happen.

CHAPTER EIGHT

THE NEW AFRICA

Tom's body froze and time went on and on, year after year and Tom still slept through the slaves being finally set free. Tom slept through the wars and the discrimination of the sixties the busing and the riots and the marches now it was year two thousand and seven and magical he was awoken by a loud noise over him. "Hey Joe this is the last piece of land we have to pile then they can start laying the cement." The white man said to his boss another white man that was in charge of taking the patch of land and getting it cleared for a shopping mall to be built on it.

    Tom heard the noise and could feel the rumbling in the ground above him and started to dig and dig until he saw light. Tom dug more until it was a good size hole and he kicked enough dirt away then climbed out of the ground. Tom's slave shirt and pants was all covered with the dirt and his feet was packed in it, he was able to clean the dirt away from his eyes but he was not ready for what he saw. All the trees were gone nothing but flat land, Tom looked around shocked wondering where he was. Then he began to run and he stopped, scared when he found himself looking at this strange place that had things he never seen before. Tom ran some more and found his self in the downtown area that was full of cars and street lights and tall buildings all around with black and white people walking up and down the street and the noises from the cars had Tom scared. Tom saw the street and tried to run across it to the other side but soon as he hit the street and saw the cars he stopped in the middle of the street shaking at the sight of these strange machines. "Where am I, and what are these strange carriages with people in them!?" Tom said to himself shocked to unbelief. Then the people in the cars stopped and got out yelling at Tom. "Get the fuck out the street nigger!" One man said "What's wrong with you, you crazy get out the street!" "You trying to get your ass ran over get out my way!" Tom was in shock not understanding a lot of what was happening so he stood there until a police car drove up.

Tom saw the car and two men in uniforms got out, it was a white man and a black man. Tom ran over to the black police officer speaking in African language being he couldn't understand this new slang language too much and hoping this black man might be from some tribe back in Africa. *"Please, help me I don't know where I am?"* Tom asked but him not knowing the police procedures when he came at the black police man, the police officer took it as an attack and grabbed him along with the help from the other officer. They cuffed his hands up behind his back; Tom was scared and was begging for help in his African language. "What's wrong with this one?" The white police man asked. "He must of got a hold of some bad drugs, lets drop him off at that coo coo house." The black one said. So they put Tom in the back of the car and drove off. Tom was so scared as he was in this strange machine and how it moved without a horse.

Later they got Tom to the mental hospital; Tom was jumping up in down, yelling trying to get away from his captors. Then they put him in this garment that tied his arms behind his back and then put him into a white room that had nothing in it, no chairs or tables. The floor and the walls were made of soft cotton. Tom was scared out of his mind he kept running his body against the door trying to get out of this nightmare. Tom pounded on the door until finally he got tired and sat down in the corner of the room scared wondering how he got to this strange land. Then two white men came in and gave him a shot of medicine calming him down.

Later a black woman in a strange garment brought him food and fed him. Tom ate and watched her, after she finished she got up to leave. "No, don't leave me!" Tom begged. "Don't worry the doctor will be in and a minute." She said. "Who is this doctor?" He asked. "He is the one that is going to help you." She said. Tom thought maybe this doctor will let him out of this place. When the white doctor came in to talk to Tom, Tom told him he was from Africa and he had run away from the plantation. The doctor nodded his head and then gave Tom another shot of medicine then left and said to the nurse. "We got a real live one, he thinks he's an African slave he didn't even know how to use a toilet!" The shots went on for a while, Tom's mind and body was so medicated he couldn't do anything but sit and stare. Finally they let him out the blank room and put him into another one with a bed and a toilet. The doctors saw Tom was showing some progress so they eased up on the medication and Tom's mind was coming back to him slowly. But nothing got him ready for the talking box and all its pictures. The things he saw on TV was amazing he would watch it as much as he could and he was starting to understand, this was not the plantation he was in another time where blacks were free and were doing everything even flying machines to the moon. Tom was scared and wondered where Melissa and his family were and he wanted to get out so he could go find them. "Man they ain't gonna let you out until you get with the program!" Roy laughed.

Roy was a patient there in the ward with Tom, he was a skinny brown skin man, who was very loud and mouthy and he took to Tom. "What is the program Roy?" Tom asked. "If you want to get out of here you better stop talking about you being a slave, we black people are all slaves but they don't want to hear that shit." Roy said. "Why are you here is your mind sick?" Tom asked. "No, I'm not crazy, I just play crazy so I wont have to go to the big house." "The big house where the white slave owners are?" Tom asked confused. "You can say that, but now they call the big house, jail and the slave owners are the police." Roy laughed. "Why would they want to put you in this jail?" Tom asked. "Because I got caught stealing at a store." "Why would you steal when you can now work and get your own, here in this land they pay you for working. Where I come from you work all day and you get nothing but a shack and they even give you the food you eat, they tell you what to wear they even tell you when to mate." Tom explained. Roy decided to humor Tom thinking this man was out of his mind. "You mean they tell you when you can get some, man you really are crazy. I know I could never had lived in a place where I was whipped, because the first time the Masa tried to hit my black ass with that whip, I would of took it and tied it around his neck!" Roy said. Tom shook his head Roy didn't have a clue about slave life, but Tom was beginning to understand to get out of this place he was to have to go along with the program. Tom was amazed how the black people worked along with the white people. The first time he saw a black woman order some white workers to work Tom cried like a baby. As the medication wore off Tom thought more about Mellissa and the baby and how he hoped he had killed the Overseer. This new place was madness and now he was in another time, where black people were free. It was a different place but he still felt the same and he still hated the white man and he still was locked up, so he did what Roy had said, told the doctors what they wanted to hear until finally the doctors approved him to be put in a halfway house that housed mental patients that was working their way back into society. The house had six one bedroom apartments five for the patients and one for the house monitor who kept the rules. Tom was taking his first steps to freedom.

CHAPTER NINE

THE BLACK WOMANS DRAMA

The first day Tom saw his new place he didn't know what to think other than this was the beginning of freedom. Tom was happy that Roy had a room at the halfway house also. "Tom we gonna get out and get this stuff hot and cracking!" Roy said excited. Tom looked at Roy like he was speaking a new language. "Never mind I just want to show you the hot spots where the women are!" "I have a woman." Tom replied. "That's in your fantasy world, she's not here and stop talking like that African or they gonna lock your black ass back up!" Roy said trying to get Tom to understand the way of the world.

That night Roy took Tom to his first outing as a free man, he took him to a bar. When they got to the club Roy's three buddies was waiting for him. There was Mo, a big black middle age man and Gary a tall fancy dress man who was very bright skin and last there was Joe a short bald brown skin man. "Say dudes what's up I want you to meet Tom, but I call him the African. I met him at the coo coo house." Roy said, They all greeted with hugs for Roy, this made Tom think of back in Africa and the elders and how they would huddle together. When the men started drinking Tom declined, he saw the white man when they got drunk and they would get mean and crazy, he saw no reason to act like that. "Man you don't drink no beer African, that's cool more for us." Mo laughed. Then the men started their conversation while Tom sat back and listen and was startled how they often used the word nigger to relate to each other. "Say man did you hear that nigga Jackson got caught selling and the Po Po gave him twenty five." Joe said. "What was he selling to get put in jail?" Tom asked and all the men looked at each other then at Roy who put his finger up to his head and turned it around in circles looking at Tom. The men laughed and figured Tom wasn't like Roy he really was crazy. "The nigga was selling heroin." Joe said. "Why would he sell drugs to make your mind sick, after being in the hospital and being shot up with these drugs I can't imagine someone wanting to be drugged?" Tom asked. "It's a high feeling, a good feeling you get African." Joe tried to explain. "But to be high means your feet is not on the ground, your mind is not level and you can't possibly focus correctly when your head is in the clouds." Tom stated. "Man it ain't that serious, chill out African!" Gary said then a curvy white woman walked by and he said.

"Ooh wee look at that fine woman, I got to get her digits!" "You mate with white women?" Tom asked surprised. "Mate, Roy your boy is crazy for real, I think he needs to go back to the ward for more treatment, and yes I mate with the white woman, a lot of them." Gary laughed. "But what of the black women?" Tom asked. "What of them, ain't nobody trying to be with those loud mouth bitches!" Gary responded then Tom's eyes went wide in anger. "How can you disrespect the black woman, do you realize how hard they have had it. They worked harder then the men sometimes because after they finished picking the cotton all day and then took care of her family, then their job was not done then they had to take care of the white men and they did not get a choice. And the black slave man couldn't do anything but watch while the white man took their women, because if we had strike back everyone would get whipped or killed. And now in this new land we can have the black women to ourselves and you choose to pass her up, it seems like she is getting disrespected all over again." Tom said sadly. The table got quiet until Gary said. "You know African you got a point, I never thought of it like that, I guess I gave our sisters a hard time."

Later as Tom and Roy were walking back to their room they started talking. "Look African we got to start this job tomorrow our case worker got for us, please don't start preaching or you will be fired the first day." Tom was excited about his first job it was minimum wage, but this time he wouldn't be working for free. The next morning the case worker was there to take the men to work. Tom was ready and at the door, but no Roy, after fifteen more minutes Tom went up to Roy's room and knocked on his door. When Roy didn't answer Tom went in and found Roy still sleeping. "Roy, Roy wake up we have a job to do!" Tom said shaking Roy to wake him up. "Man what time is it?" Roy asked all groggy. "It is six thirty and we have only thirty minutes to get to our new job." Tom said nervously because he remembered back on the plantation you had when the sun came up to be on the fields and if you were late you got beat. "I ain't going today, tell the man I'll go tomorrow." Roy said and rolled back in bed. Tom got upset then pulled his blanket off of him. "No, Roy you will go to work today, you have a opportunity to work for your own money so you can buy anything you want, that's freedom, but you chose to ignore this chance and continue to be a slave to the white man. Having him feed and clothed you, no Roy, you are my only friend in this new land and I won't let you be a slave to the white man like I had been for so long." Tom said shaking so upset. "Okay African but don't ever come in here again pulling the blanket off of me again, or we gonna have a problem. I didn't let my ex-wife make me go to work." Roy said. "Maybe that is why she is your EX wife." Tom said. "You know African if I didn't know any better I would think you was making a joke." Roy laughed. "No Roy I would not make fun of you not having a woman or a job." Tom said and left the room.

And those words hit Roy hard, no woman and no job. Tom was right he didn't have either and it wasn't funny. Roy thought about that while he was getting up and how he never graduated from high school always hanging with his home boys, so he couldn't get a job so he then would find a desperate sister and live with her until finally he met Karen. Karen was a beautiful black sister that he wanted to be with, but she was one of those sisters that you had to bring it or not be up in her face. So Roy got a job and married her and they had two children and he was doing the family thing until he started putting his home boys over his family. Roy was hanging out at the club later and later getting drunk and messing with what the fellows called the bar bitches. These women spent most of their time at the bars, trying to get free drinks and picking up some ones husband. No man took them serious because they knew the next day they would be back at the same bar waiting for the next drink and the next man. And the men knew that's all they were good for, you give them a few drinks and they give you a night of sex and the bar bitches was cheaper than the hoes. Roy got messed up with them and hanging out with his buddies so much that he couldn't get up and go to work in the morning. So eventually he got fired and Karen tried to hold on even though she had a home and two children and now a husband to take care of on one salary. Roy would hang out so much he wouldn't get up in the morning to go look for a job. So Karen finally did what she had to, she put him out and he remembered the last thing she said to him. "A man doesn't need to be told to get up and work and take care of his family, he just does it, when you turn back into that man you come back." After that Roy not wanting to work got into stealing to have money and he was getting by until he got caught. Roy faked like he was crazy to get out of going to jail. Now he was faced with either working or going back into the life of stealing, he knew it was time for him to wake up.

That morning the two fellows entered the bean factory, it was a summer job so their case worker set it up for Roy and Tom to work. Roy also forty years of age didn't like the ideal of working on the factory line picking bad beans off the belt, but it was a job. Tom on the other hand was looking forward to working for money. The boss had told Roy and Tom what the job consist of and was about to lead them to the sorting line when another white boss came in and said someone didn't come in and they needed a strong man to stack cases off the line. They both looked at skinny Roy and shook their heads no, but Tom he was huge from working the field his muscles was all over his body. So Tom got the job to stack cases with this white fellow whose name was Kirk who was a big built white man who tried to shake Tom's hand when the boss brought him over. Tom looked at him not offering his hand thinking. "I will work beside you white man, but that is all."

Tom was told that he and Kirk was to stack cases as they came down the line, it was a hard job that took two people and sometimes three to keep up and keep the line running. So after Tom was told the set up he began helping Kirk stacking cases, in between stacking Kirk tried to strike up a conversation with Tom but only got a mean stare. "If it is not part of the job to speak to the white man, then I choose not too!" Tom said to himself and continued to stack cases. The job was so easy to Tom that Kirk would stop working and just watch this black man do the job of two men. So Kirk decided to sneak off and take a coffee break, he saw that Tom wasn't going to complain about being left to do all the work, so Kirk left. As the time went by people came by and saw Tom stacking those cases by himself. Some of the black workers was getting upset and called the boss then the floor boss walked by and saw Tom handling this job with ease. He couldn't believe it and then told his boss. The white people enjoyed this, less work for them, the black's did not. "What you trying to do nigga, out there working like a slave you making it bad for all the rest of us!" One black worker yelled at Tom and Roy while they were having lunch. "What do you mean, making you look bad, what am I doing wrong?" Tom asked surprised. "You're doing the job of two men, they gonna expect us black men to be able to do all that hard work while the white man gets the easy jobs!" Another black worker yelled and at this time now it was a whole table of angry black people there. "Oh boy African what have you done now." Roy thought watching all these angry black faces. "I am sorry to upset you my brothers and sisters but where I come from, I was use to working hard, that is all I know. I did not have the opportunities like you have to go to school and get this education to get a job to use my brain, but I am a strong proud black African man and my father taught me to always do your best, I can do no less. But one thing I am learning there is many opportunities in this land and you can do what you want if you work hard so maybe one day you will be the one walking around giving orders instead of working the lines." The black workers left wondering where this man came from who just gave them some shade and Tom's words had them thinking.

Later as the two men was returning home Roy asked Tom. "African what do you plan to do with all that money you will make?" "I plan to save enough to go back home to Africa." Tom said proudly. "Man you crazy, this is Africa, New Africa and you said it best our ancestors worked hard and built this land. My mama and daddy and their mama and daddy and so on, all was raised here. We didn't ask to come here. I can't imagine the Africans standing by the ocean with tickets to ride over here to work their asses off, no I don't think so. So we are here and if the white man don't like it he shouldn't have came over and got our black asses. Man I can see it now if things was different me and my boys would all be sitting under some trees in Africa playing dominos and drinking coconut milk watching the sisters walking around with their tities out, but no here I am working for six dollars an hour, it's the shits but we're here." Roy replied. Tom thought to his self he knew full well of the ride over and all the death and the struggles the black people endured by being brought here, so why leave when it was so many opportunities. Tom learned of black millionaires and now there was even a black man running for President of this land, no there was no need to go back to Africa. The black slaves gave so much to build this new land, now it is time to take, and Tom was ready to take and now be a free man in this New Africa. Weeks had gone by and Tom was learning more and more of this New Africa, he continued to work hard at his job. Everyone was in awe of this proud black man and how he brought it everyday, working hard. Charles the house monitor was observing how Tom was doing well always ready to work, always back at home on time. Tom cause no trouble the only thing he could tell is that Tom didn't care much for him, only speaking when he had to. And it was too bad because Charles was a good middle age white man who had a black wife of over twenty years and three children. Charles had got into the medical field when he was younger when he watched his father who slipped into mental illness when he was a boy leaving his mother and him to fend for themselves. Charles was a good man and also a Christian man who wanted to help, but to Tom he was a white man who was just like the ones that killed his family and hurt everyone he ever loved.

After a while Tom was going to work and hanging out with Roy and getting Americanized and lots of the things Tom saw hurt him to watch like some of his people not seizing the opportunity this land had for them now. Tom learned of so many of the black men in jail, and selling drugs and the women on the streets prostituting was heartbreaking but the worst was the gangs. Tom would walk the streets and see the young boys cussing and fighting with their own kind, he couldn't believe they could turn out so cruel. Tom wished he could take the gangs all back to the plantation one day and let them work side by side in the hot sun and only having that black slave to lean on to cry with. Back in the day when one slave got whipped and the others would have to watch it was like they were all getting whipped too, feeling every swap, but now here in this land they were hurting each other. "How could this be!" Tom cried just thinking of the shame his father would have on his face to see how sad some of the young black men and women had become. Roy seeing the sad look on Tom's face decided to take him out to the bar with him. "Look Tom, I know you don't care for the bar much, but you need to get out and socialize." Roy said. So Tom agreed to go with Roy who reminded him of his friend Obadele back in Africa.

When the two men got to the bar the gang was all there. Gary, Mo and Joe and right away Roy joined in with the fellows drinking up a storm. Tom watched and knew he would have to almost fight to get Roy up for work in the morning. The men was all talking and laughing and drinking when this brown skin curvy woman with lots of makeup on her face and had on a short top that exposed most of her breast and a mini skirt that didn't cover all her bottom walked in the club. Tom was shock, back in Africa wearing less clothing was accepted but not in this new land and when the other men saw his face they all started laughing. "Look African, you don't want none of that, that's Molly we call her hot tamale, she's a hoe." Roy said. "Yeah she probably got more diseases in her than a lab rat!" Joe laughed. Tom watched how no one wanted to talk to her, and then the owner had put her out. Tom feeling sorry for her got up to go after her. "Man if you touch that you better put two rubbers on your Johnson!" Mo laughed.

Tom got outside and found Molly standing on the corner smoking a cigarette, he then walked up to her. Molly looked up and saw Tom coming and said. "It's twenty for a blow, fifty for a full job and a thousand for all night, what you want?" She asked with no emotion. "I just want to talk to you my sister." Tom said sincerely. Molly looked at him. "Talk you crazy, get away from me!" Molly yelled. "I don't want to hurt you, I want to know why you are hurting yourself?" Tom asked. "What you mean hurting myself I make five hundred dollars sometimes a grand a night, I bet you don't make that much nigga!" "No I don't I make minimum wage." Tom stated. "Then I know you need to get out of my face!" Molly yelled and began to walk away. "Don't you know you're special." Tom said. Molly stopped in her tracks. No one has ever said that to her. "What do you mean special, you don't know me!" "I know you're a beautiful black woman and you don't realize it. You know I have seen so many black women misused and there was a time she didn't have a choice to give out her treasure, it was taken from her. Now to give it away for mere money is a shame it is worth more than that, more than gold and diamonds. Back where I come from the young men in our village would have to fight lions and climb mountains just to be able to get to the treasure." Tom expressed. "Where you come from, here we sisters have to work what we got to survive you see there ain't many black men stepping up. Their either in jail, selling drugs gay or with the white women, there ain't nothing left for us. I was brought up in an abusive home and I didn't go to school I had to work and the only thing I got is this body!" She cried. "And that is too precious to sell my sister, many years later when you get older you don't want to look back on your life and see that this was all you could do in life." He said. "This is all I know." She responded sadly. "Then learn something else." Tom said. "But I have been doing this shit so long what does it matter!" Molly said frustrated. "There was a saying I heard that, you do better when you know better, now you know." Tom said. Molly looked at him and something he said penetrated to her heart. "Yes I do know better, thank you." Molly said walking away knowing that this stranger made her feel different about herself, and if he can see something good in her, maybe there is and she had to see for herself and she walked off the streets for good. Tom felt good about what he had done and wondered why so many black women was so unhappy and when he met Sara she showed him the reason why.

CHAPTER TEN

RASING A GROWN MAN

Tom had met Sara one day on one of his walks when he had passed by her house and saw Sara a full figure, light skin short hair woman that was outside her house trying to cut her grass. Tom laughed to himself how she was trying but wasn't getting very far. Tom walked pass then he had to turn around. "Miss would you like me to help you with that?" Tom asked. Sara looked up at this dark built handsome man and thought she was dreaming. "No, I think I got it. She replied. "Are you sure I don't mind helping." Tom offered. Sara was so tooken back by his generosity and being tired she finally said yes and allowed Tom to cut her grass, which he did easily. "Wow, you done already this would of took me all day to finish, here I don't have much but I can pay you ten dollars." She said trying to hand him the money. "Oh no, Miss I don't want your money, I just wanted to help." Tom said. "I must of died and gone to heaven, I haven't had a man do anything for me in a long time. My lazy son he lives here, but I can't get him to do anything, thank you so much sir." Sara replied happily. "My name is Tom and it was a pleasure, a beautiful woman like yourself should not have to do man's work." "What! and Where did you come from and my name is Sara." She said smiling her white teeth at him. Tom thought about it and didn't want to scare her off so he told her he was from Africa but not when he came from there. "Well I got to pay you something, I hope your hungry because I cooked a big dinner and I would like to share it with you for being so kind."

After coming in and eating a huge meal Sara told Tom how she was fifty years old and she had a thirty four year old son named Trey and a thirty three year old daughter named Tomeka. Sara's story was sad she had got pregnant and had her son at sixteen then her daughter at seventeen. Their father was a gang banger and got into a gang fight and shot another gang banger and was put in jail. Unfortunately Trey her son wanted to take after his father and was now in a gang also. Tomeka her daughter started even earlier than Sara having her first child at thirteen then she had three more all from different men.

Sara didn't know why she was telling this man all her business but for so long she had been by herself and wishing and hoping and praying for a NICE black man to come into her life, but all she kept getting was the lazy ones that wanted to lay up on her in her house while she worked and he would stay home thinking all he had to do is screw her good. Sara thought she hoped she never came across a man that could screw her that good to make her be that crazy, but she had to admit she was getting lonely and Tom seem like a nice man and he had a job. They talked more than Tom told her his situation and that he had to go back to his place. The thought of Tom living in a half way house for mental people bothered her for a little while, then she thought of all those crazy men she had already got hooked up with, and Tom didn't look or talk crazy so she then made a date to meet again. Tom was having such a good time with this woman he had over looked the time, when he got back to the halfway house he was a few minutes late.

When Tom came in the door Charles was sitting there talking with a black woman. Tom was nervous back at the plantation if you was late you got whipped. "I am sorry, sir I am late." Tom said with his head down but was shocked at Charles' response. "No problem Tom, you have never gave me any problems, so if you're a few minutes late its okay, I trust you not to be late often." "What kind of white man is this?" Tom thought to himself in shock. Then the black woman got up. "Charles where is your manners, I'm Gloria Charles' wife, he tells me you're a good man." Then she went to shake Tom's hand Tom was shocked and the smile on her face as she reached out her hand to him, she surprised him, he was not use to this. Black women with white men, don't they realize how, they were taken from the black man, now they give themselves up freely, this truly was a strange time. Gloria shook Tom's hand and then offered him some cake she had brought over to her husband. Tom thanked them and walked up to his room in shock, later he told Roy what happen. "Please Tom don't get it twisted, there are some nice white folks around but you still got those ones that will smile in your face shake your hand then stab you in the back. Some are nice because they want to be and then you got the ones that are nice because they have to." Tom had saw on TV about the Ku Klux Klan and just figured it was Overseers and slave Masters reduced to now having to cover their heads in shame. This time was surly different when some whites had changed to the better and some blacks had changed to the worst.

Days later Tom had went by to visit Sara; it was a Saturday so they had the day off. Tom learned that Sara had gone to school later after having her children and got a degree to be an executive secretary. Sara had been working at her job for over ten years and was upset how she watched the other white women being promoted over her. "Well I guess all things haven't changed." Tom thought as his heart broke thinking that some black sisters was still in slavery always giving, but still locked up in despair. So for Sara this was a great day for her. Tom was respectful, polite and very attentive to her. "This man must be from mars, cause I ain't never seen a man so sweet, I got to lock this one up." Sara thought to herself smiling back at Tom. After the two had went to the park then to a movie Sara invited Tom back to her home for dinner, hoping he was hungry for dinner and for her.

When they got to her house Tom offered to help her in the kitchen to cook, he was enjoying every minute with Sara and even though he missed Melissa he knew, she was no longer around and he had to move on, his heart, mind and body was telling him he had to move on. Sara declined his offer and told him to "Sit down and watch TV, you cut the grass, I'll cook the food." She reminded him of Asante back in Africa. Tom sat there in the living room happy watching TV when this young black man came busting in the house. "Nigga what you doing sitting up in my crib!" The man cussed. Tom stood up then Sara came running out the kitchen. "Trey, this is Tom my new friend, Tom this is my son Trey." Tom looked at this young man his pants was hanging past his butt with his belt fasten around it, he was wearing a t-shirt and you could see all the tattoos on his body Trey had diamonds everywhere, on his ears fingers in his watch and in the gold chains he wore around his neck. Tom wondered often why the black man wore sagging pants because he remembered how as a slave you wore what the Master gave you and when your clothes hung off your body it was because you got beat out of them. And Tom had seen enough chains in his lifetime there was no way Tom was gonna wear another and the tattoos he had plenty marks on his body from the whip no way would he add another. Tom was not impressed with Trey, he was rude to his mother then he walked in the kitchen and ate food right out the pot, then went downstairs where his room was at. Tom could see the embarrassment in Sara's face. "Are you okay would you like to sit down and talk?" Tom asked her. Sara was overtaken by the sweetness of this man; she sat down and bared her soul. Sara told Tom that Trey was thirty four years old and dropped out of school, and was always in trouble with the law, he had got into a gang early and once a rival gang came by and shot at their house. "Trey don't want to get a job and work he just want to live off of me, but what can I do, he's my son." She said sadly. "Yes but even a mama bird has to push her baby bird out to see if he can fly." Tom said trying to explain. "Yeah I guess Trey ain't ready to fly." She said. "Maybe you're not ready to give him a push." Tom said striking a nerve. Tom was finding out that some black sons that were still in there thirties was still living at home and their mothers could find no wrong in them, always making excuses for their sons even if their out there dealing drugs, gang banging or disrespecting ladies it was always someone else's fault. It seems to Tom like the black woman would never get out of slavery first it was to the white man now it was to her children.

Tom went home sad for Sara and he thought Trey had problems that was bad, until he came face to face with Sara's daughter Tomeka. Tomeka had came over one afternoon with her four children and it looked like she was with child again. "No, Tomeka please tell me you're not pregnant again!" Sara asked upset and she loved her grandchildren but Tomeka's oldest son was twenty and like his Uncle Trey he stayed at home with her in her three bedroom section eight house. At eighteen Tomeka got on welfare and had been living like that every since. Now at thirty three she had dropped out of school to have her babies then had to stay home and keep them, because Sara had to work to feed her and Trey and now her grandchildren. Finally Tomeka moved out and got her own place and had never worked a job, that didn't sit well with Sara. Sara had her kids young but she still got a job to take care of them, but Tomeka chose not to work and take the easy route, but what could Sara do, Tomeka was her child and at lease she wasn't living at the house like

Trey. Tomeka looked Tom up and down, jealous her mama had a man and now she didn't. "Mama don't you think you're a little bit too old to be dating?" She laughed trying to be funny, but make a point also. "No, I don't but what I do know is your gonna have a problem finding you a man with all those kids hanging around." Sara said also trying to be funny and make a point. "What ever!" Tomeka said sarcastically. "I just came by to borrow some money they gonna cut my lights off tomorrow." She said. Tom got up and walked out the room trying not to interfere in Sara's private business with her daughter. "What's his problem?" Tomeka asked. "Nothing he's a good man and he didn't want to hear you begging for money. Tomeka don't mess this up for me, I really like this man!" Sara pleaded with her. "Please mama he ain't any different from any other man he just want to get some then he's gonna be gone." "No, child that's all the boys you mess with, this is a man, a good one and I'm damn lucky to get him, when it's so few good ones available." Sara said. "Well anyway you gonna help me with my lights or not?" Tomeka asked rudely like Sara was suppose to do this. "No I aint got no money, I got my own bills to pay." Sara said. "Okay when they turn off the lights we will all be back here to live with you, I don't think your new man would like that." Tomeka laughed. Sadly Sara went into her room to find the money.

Tomeka walked out into the living room and saw Tom sitting on the couch with her two young children. Tee Tee that was four and Derrick that was five. Tom's heart was melting watching these two children and glad they didn't have to grow up in slavery where the children as soon as they could work was put out on the fields. These children today were free to go to school and be anything they wanted. Tears started to form in Tom's eyes as he talked to these children. Tomeka was behind them and was overwhelmed watching her mother's man bonding with her children something their daddies never did. Tomeka story was being a young girl without a father and a mother that was working all the time she felt alone and was looking for attention so she found it in this twenty year old street punk. Shortly after her first young son Michael was born then Trina came a year later. Then she got pregnant again and had an abortion, hardly able to take care of the two, and then years later she had her younger two and now she was pregnant again by a one night stand. Tomeka not wanting to work and these kids even though she loved them they were also her income. But now she was scared even though her life was gone she didn't want Trina to live like her, never having a life only having and taking care of babies. No school, no job, no study man and she knew by the way her mama looked at her she was ashamed of her. That look often gave Tomeka the "I don't care" attitude. Deep in thought she didn't see Trey enter the house.

"What you here for to get more money from mama, wont you get money from all those nigga's you keep having all these babies by!" Trey shouted. "What you worried about me getting money from mama, what do you think you're doing, living here. You get money every day she pays to keep a roof over your head she feeds you and pays for the water to wash your sorry ass. What do you pay, nothing you live here for free at least I got my own place nigga!" Tomeka yelled. "That's because your job is lying on your back!" Trey yelled back. "Fuck you Trey!" Tomeka yelled and jumped in his face. "Look, don't go jumping in my face!" Trey told her then pushed her back, and then from the other room Tomeka's son Michael came out the room raising his shirt up and was pointing at a pistol in his pants. "We got a problem here Unk, we got a problem!" Michael yelled also in a rival gang on the other side. "Young nigga you from the other set and the only reason I tolerate your ass is because of mama but don't get it twisted, if you don't get out of my face, it's gonna be a funeral up in here!" Trey yelled reaching for his gun, and then Sara hearing all the noise ran into the room scared and upset then Tom jumped up and yelled.

"Stop this madness!" "Look nigga you better get your nose out of this, this is family business!" Michael yelled. "Is this how families treat each other now, how can you disrespect this woman and your grandmother who loves all of you in her own house, and what about the babies here or you going to shoot each other right in front of them. Think my young brothers, this is not what families are about." Tom said so shock how these black people treated each other back in Africa or on the plantation he never saw family go at each other like this. Sara had tears in her eyes thinking if their father could have had just a little of this man's integrity, maybe her kids would have turned out better. Tomeka being scared for her son, but was in awe of this man and could see why her mother liked this man now wishing that if just one of her babies daddies could had been like this man. Trey on the other hand thinking he was the man of the house didn't appreciate Tom interfering. "Nigga for mama's sake this is the one and only time I'm gonna let you get away with jumping in my business, next time it's gonna be a man down situation." Then he left. Tom stood there feeling bad how this young fellow was so lost and he wasn't going to be satisfied until he was dead and Tom wondered if Sara could see all this.

Later after Trey left and everything settled down Tomeka sat down by Tom to talk. "I'd like to thank you for what you did today, my son Michael is just like Trey both hard headed and angry, both pulling out guns in the house. Maybe if Michael had a father around him he wouldn't act so stupid!" Tomeka said upset. "Please Tomeka don't take offense of what I want to say, but Trey is old, but Michael is young and if you don't want him to turn out like his Uncle you have to help him out this vicious cycle." "What am I suppose to do, Michael is near grown and my daughter Trina…." Then Tomeka stopped and started to cry. "I don't want my baby girl to live like me, I want her to go to school get a job and have a husband and then have children after she has her life together, but what can I say, how can I tell her to be better than me!" She cried. "Just like that, tell her you expect her to do better and then you might have to move yourself away from these bad elements. Surround your children around other children that's hungry for success, and that wants all this land has to offer, tell Trina she can be the next Oprah if she wants. Tell Michael he can do anything even run for President it's all out there for them to grab, but you have to let them see it, don't let them fail to get all that is available to them." Tom said. Tomeka had tears in her eyes and she hugged Tom like a daughter would to her father, and before she left she told her mother. "Mama, whatever you do don't let that man go, he's a keeper. I'm gonna try to relocate and get my kids away from this nightmare. I got to try, if I don't do anything else in my life and then I might even go back to school. I got to do better by my kids, and I am not blaming you anymore for how I was raised. I just want more for mine and I'm sorry for all the trouble I caused you." Tomeka cried. Sara held her daughter and was thinking how Tomeka didn't have a chance at thirteen she was made a mother but she was still a child. Sara was so busy trying to keep a roof over her kids head that, she had over looked what was going in them. Now both her kids were older and now she was feeling like she had failed them.

Later that night Tom and Sara sat by the fireplace. "Tom I'm sorry for what you saw today, sometimes my children can get out of hand, if only I had a man to help raise them, but I didn't so I had to work and somehow the streets raised them, and now I think it's too late." Sara said sadly. "Maybe, maybe not, the way I feel as long as you are free you have a chance to change. You did the best you could I just wish you wasn't by yourself trying to be the mother and father." Tom said then looked in her eyes and began to kiss her. Tom could feel himself getting aroused and he enjoyed this beautiful proud black woman and Sara was thinking this man was a dream come true and they were getting lost in each others arms when Trey busted in. "Nigga you still here, ain't it time for you to check back in at the coo coo house, You know you got to get your rest so you can go to that penny ante job you got!" Trey yelled. Sara was so embarrassed she had told Trey about Tom, and where he was living and that he had a job not to put him down but to tell her son about the man she wanted in her life, hoping that Trey would grow to at least respect the man. "Stop Trey this is my house and my friend!" Sara yelled. "Mama that nigga is just trying to move up in here!" Trey yelled. Tom got up off the couch and told Trey "I think it would be too hard for me as a man to live in a house with a boy pretending to be one!" Tom said getting upset. "What you saying I ain't no man!" Trey yelled jumping in Tom's face. Sara jumped up and got between them. "I'm saying where I come from you had to prove yourself to be a man there was a journey you had to take, you son have not took that journey yet." Tom said then left trying not to disrupt Sara's home.

Sara sat down on the couch and cried thinking that her grown son again has stopped her chances of being happy. "Why do you do this Trey, don't you want me to be happy, you want me to be alone the rest of my life, oh no I forgot you'll always be here, Hun son, you're so selfish." Sara said then got up walked to her bedroom and closed the door. Trey was feeling bad now for his mother and had tears in his eyes thinking how he didn't want to hurt her, but this was what it was. Trey was thirty four, a drop out, with a criminal record, and no one was trying to hire his black ass, and why would he want to work for peanuts like Tom, when he can sell his drugs and make big money. And if his mama didn't like what he was doing she shouldn't accept the money he made from it. "That nigga ain't no good all he wants to do is come up here, play big man of the house then break her heart. Then she will come running to me to put things back together, no, I'm the man of this house here, mama will get over this." Trey said to his self and then went down stairs to his room.

CHAPTER ELEVEN

COTTON FIELDS TO JAIL HOUSE

Tom walked back home upset that Sara was a proud woman but let her son be so disrespectful. "What have the black man turned into beast, trying to kill each other like animals!" Tom said to his self then he got to the park outside his home and saw the strangest thing, little black and white kids playing together laughing and having fun. Tom also saw a couple a black man and a white woman walk down the street hand and hand, it was like Charles and Gloria and the children they didn't see color, this was definitely a new time were people that had changed some for the good and some for the bad.

The next few days after work Roy invited Tom to join him and the fellows at the bar and being Tom didn't want any problems with Sara and her son he decided to go along, Tom had stopped going by Sara's house, to Sara's heartbreak. "So African haven't seen you around lately where you been?" Joe asked. "Tom got him a woman." Roy laughed. "What she let you have the night off to hang with the boys?" Gary asked. "No I was having a few problems with her son." Tom answered. "What the little dude kept blocking." Mo laughed. "No and he is not that young." Tom said. "How old is he?" Joe asked. "Trey is thirty four years old." "Oh hell no!" All of the men said together. "What is wrong?" Tom asked. "You know some black women always crying about us black men, and how we chose the white women, or we in jail on drugs and how few there is to choose from, but when we do give a sister a chance, then what happens fella's?" Gary asked. "You got baby drama!" Mo said. "What are you talking about it is honorable for a woman to take care of her children." Tom stated. "Yeah when they are young but not those grown ass men, in their thirties still living at home. I was with this one sister and she had a son in his thirties sitting at home and me and the woman was trying to kick it, but I couldn't take it, the little nigga was walking around the house like he was the man of the house. Eating my food and every time me and the woman got in a argument the little nigga would get in my face telling me he was gonna whoop my ass, so I told the bitch I had to go she already had a man." Joe said. "I think they like to keep their sons around so they won't be alone and when the young dude start liking a woman the mama talk about the girl so bad and run her off. So then the young dude is stuck at home with mama and she don't care because she ain't got no man and don't want to be alone!" Gary added. Then all the men started laughing except for Tom. "Tom, don't worry about it, if the woman want to take care of the grown ass nigga all his life, then let her!" Roy said.

Tom looked at the men and finally lost it he got up and started yelling everyone in the bar stopped to listen. "You know since I have been here in this strange land and I have heard you men call each other and yourself nigga so many times I can't count, and I fail to understand how you can say that to each other!" Tom yelled finally fed up. "Calm down, Tom we don't call each other that to hurt each other or put us down we use what the white man used to call us as a term of endearment. Like he's my nigga or nigga please, we say it because they can't!" Roy tried to explain. "No Roy, that word will never ever be a term of endearment, if you realize how hurtful and painful it sounded to the slaves and later in the sixty's where black people was called this horrible name. Don't you know some white people still think of us as nigga's and they would call us that but can't but they get enjoyment when you call each other that because that's what they want to say and how they feel. At the beginning the white men would whip the slaves and shout nigger, then they would yell pick that cotton nigger does any of that sound like a term of endearment. That word was used to keep the black people down and as long as you use it you will be doing the same thing, we are people and we are free and I choose not to be a nigger!" Tom stated then walked out the club. "Roy, what's up with your boy?" Joe asked. "He's a proud black African American man!" Roy responded with a smile on his face.

When Tom walked back home he was so confused. "Why am I here, look what the world has come to for us slaves. I don't know what's worse watching the slave Master beating us down or seeing our own kind do it." Tom thought and when he walked in the door he saw Sara sitting there with Charles having coffee. "Hello Tom you see you have a visitor and I don't mind saying a very nice lady, if I wasn't already spoken for you might have had some competition." He laughed. "Hello, Tom I was missing you and I hope I didn't embarrass myself by coming over." She said. "No, it is a pleasant surprise, I have not been by because I thought it would be better to keep the peace in your house." Tom said. "No before I could get peace in, I had to get the problem out." She said. "What do you mean Sara?" Tom asked. "I told Trey to get out, you see Tom I felt like I failed him. I wasn't there to watch him grow up much working all the time and the streets got him. Then after so long it was too late, he was a grown man with nothing, no schooling or job skills no father and because of that I felt I failed. I let him stay home and I took care of him, he was my problem, my fault, but after you left I started thinking I wasn't doing either one of us any good by letting him waste away in my house and once I'm gone where would he be. Trey wasn't going to grow to be a man he could be and I wasn't going to have happiness in my life so I did us both a favor and kicked him out, and now I'm here to start my happiness with you." Sara said. "I don't know what to say." Tom replied. "Don't say nothing just go with her." Charles said. "But it is almost time to be in for lock down?" Tom said. "Tom love doesn't just help the heart it's good for the mind you go with this nice lady and we will call this out house treatment and I'll see you in the morning." Charles said smiling. Tom looked at this white man total overwhelmed. "Thank you Charles!" Tom said and shook his hand and it felt the same as shaking a black mans it was just a different color. That night Tom and Sara had a beautiful night of love making and Charles was right that was just what Tom needed, he felt good and alive.

That morning Sara got up she was on cloud nine that African man brought it home it was like he really appreciated this woman and was in to pleasing her and she couldn't believe how good she felt she then began cooking breakfast for this wonderful man when Tomeka came by with Tee Tee and Derrick. Derrick ran into Tom's arms it was like he was hungry for a father figure. Tom held him and took him and Tee Tee in the living room and started telling them an old African tale, about the lions and all the animals in the jungle. "Mama this man is good for you and the whole family." Tomeka said. "Thanks baby and I hope he stays around, because I haven't felt this alive in years!" Sara said and exhaled. "Mama that's why I'm here to tell you I'm leaving this town, so my kids can have a chance to have a good life and see if I can find what you got." Tomeka laughed. Then they both hugged and everything was fine until Trey came busting in the house.

"So mama, that's why you kicked me out, so you could bring this nigga in!" Trey yelled. "No, I kicked you out so you could be a man and find your own house, baby I love you but you need to start your own life!" Sara cried. "Well I ain't going nowhere this is my house too!" He said then pushed Sara aside to try to go downstairs. Tomeka jumped up and ran toward Trey. "Don't you put your hands on mama!" Trey then pushed her aside; Tom jumped up and caught Trey by the neck with his two hands and pint him up against the wall. Trey tried to get loose but Tom was too strong. "What manner of animal are you, that you would harm your own mother and sister. Your mother bore you raised you, fed and clothed you and now you try to afflict pain to her. You're worst then any slave Master I've ever seen!" Tom shouted. Trey was stuck pint against the wall and was forced by this man to really see himself and he didn't like what he saw. "I'm sorry mama, I feel lost. I'm so tired of the gangs and the fights and the drugs. I see you going to work everyday and I'm so proud of you and ashamed of myself, but I would never want to hurt you, I'm just tired!" Trey said exhausted then the tears came from his eyes. Tom let him go as Sara and Tomeka held him.

"Trey I think you just began your journey to be a man." Tom said then everyone heard Blam, Blam gun shots, everyone looked around and they saw Tee Tee in the living room but no Derrick. Tomeka yelled where is Derrick then everyone ran outside and Derrick was lying on the porch with blood coming out of his chest. "No! My baby!" Tomeka screamed Trey then ran and went to pick him up and moved him inside. Tom watched as the car with the shooter rode by again firing another shot. Everyone got down on the ground but Tom with all his anger went after the shooter and with all his African experience he ran like he was in the jungle. Tom moved around cars jumped on hoods then pounced on the top of the shooter's car. The driver was so scared he stopped the car and jumped out and ran off. Tom then jumped down and yanked this young boy out, he couldn't have been any older than twenty years old. Tom had his hands around this boys neck choking him, visualizing Derrick lying on that porch with blood coming out of him. "How could you, a little boy, your own kind!" Tom shouted and as he was choking the boy he thought is this why I am here to see how bad it was going to get for us slaves." Then the police arrived. "Back away now or we'll shoot!" The officer yelled to Tom. Tom thought I should let him kill me, watching this madness in this new land was worst then the plantation. But something made him back up and release the terrified boy. The police handcuffed Tom arrested him and took him to jail, so here was Tom locked up in this small cell wondering what was next.

Later Tom was surprised when this young black man walked into his cell. "Tom Brooks I'm your lawyer, my name is Jasper Owens I'll be helping you get out of here." "How is the boy?" Tom asked. "Derrick is in the hospital in critical condition, their doing the best they can for him, now I got to do the best for you. I don't think it will be much of a problem being that you were choking another black gang thug, now if it was a white man you would be in the hole and they would have thrown away the key. They don't care about us hurting each other they just want you off the streets before you hurt one of them." The young man explained. Tom was in awe of this man thinking how awesome a black man that turned the system around and used it to his advantage, he wasn't going to jail he was trying to get people out. "Now Tom you will have to stay here until trial, because the court cant find too much information on you, so they said you have to stay behind bars, but don't worry I'll get you out, just be careful in here and don't get in any more trouble while you're here." Mr. Owens said. "What does he mean trouble, I am already locked up". Tom thought then saw what he meant and it brought tears to his eyes to see so many black men all in their jail house gear "Is this what has come to the black slave from the cotton fields to the jail house, is this what we have in store for us." Tom thought to his self then went back in his cell to shed more tears.

The next day Tom was told by the guard to get out his cell to eat. Tom looked at the food they called breakfast and thought it was worst then that slop they served to him on the slave ship. As Tom sat down a few more black men sat down at his table. "Man, what they lock you up for?" One jailer asked. "I got into a fight with a young boy who rode by and shot down a little boy." Tom said. "Oh a drive by, what set was he from?" The man asked. "What do you mean set?" Tom asked confused. "What gang, each gang got a set and a territory they run, usually they go by shooting at rival gangs so they don't come and try to take over their territory." The man explained. "What territory all I seen is a area full of broken-down houses, filthy streets drug addicts and women walking the street selling there treasures, that is what they are trying to keep people from taking over. I don't understand why they would want to risk their lives and kill others over a place where I would want to get out." Tom expressed. "Man, it's the principal." One said. "To want to live in crime invested filth, no it's not principal its crazy." Tom said. "Well it's better than being locked up in here." Another inmate said. "Oh this ain't so bad it's three hot's and a cot!" One said. "What, has it got so bad for the black man that jail looks good?" Tom asked. "Yeah I tried to work, but no one would give me a job, and the sisters today ain't letting you live off of them anymore, they rather "be by they damn self" so what's a man to do. I stole until I got caught and put in here, now I got a roof over my head and food to eat." One jailer replied. "But what about your freedom?" Tom asked. "Freedom, man please a black man ain't free and we never gonna be free and what's out there anyway, if it was more positive places out there growing up for us black people maybe you wouldn't see so many of us in here!" A jailer expressed. "So I hear the excuses but what about the solutions?" Tom asked. "What solutions, man where you from, this is what it is!" One said. "No, this can't be, this is only one place back on the plantation everywhere was jail. Everywhere you went, no matter how far the slave went he was in jail!" Tom tried to explain but was so confused he couldn't figure out for the life of him after years of slavery how a black man with all this opportunities could go back to the same situation. locked up in chains, but the worst thing was to listen to these men talk about how many times they have been locked up and how hard they were. "Yes one swap from the Overseers whip and your flesh start melting off your body like butter then these young thugs would be crying like a baby." Tom thought to himself then walked back to his cell.

   The next day Tom was taken to the Judge and he almost fell over when he saw a black woman sitting up there in her robe. Tears fell from his eyes as Tom sat by his black lawyer and he was feeling so proud. "Mr. Brooks are you okay?" The Judge asked. "Yes your Judgeship, I am well." Tom said wiping his eyes. Then his lawyer got up and explained to the Judge that Tom had reacted in a heated situation when he attacked the young man that shot his friends grandson." "Please Mr. Owens the defendant tried to kill the man, this is attempted murder!" The Prosecutor said. "Your honor Mr. Brooks is not a violent man he has no history of crime." Mr. Owens replied "Mr. Owens he has no history, why is it his record only goes back to last year?" The Judge asked. "That's because before that he was sick and placed in a mental home where he forgot everything before that time." The young lawyer explained. "Well he's only been here a short time and already he tried to strangle a young man!" The Prosecutor said. "Young man, that young man shot at a house with a family in it and shot down a little boy that's fighting for his life as we speak now. Mr. Brooks is a good man and there are a few people here to speak in his defense." The lawyer replied.

Tom turned around and saw Sara, Tomeka, Roy and Charles and his wife Gloria. First up was Sara who had been crying her eyes all red as she told the Judge that Tom was a real good man and he tried to help with her kids to try to show them it's better ways and opportunities out there, and that she had wished she had met him sooner because he would have been a good father to her kids and maybe they would of turned out better. Next up was Roy. "I met Tom in the coo coo house but I don't think he belonged there his mind is focus on freedom for our people. Tom is different, he's always trying to school us dudes he even got us to stop saying nig….- oh I mean the N word. He got me getting up working everyday, and he works very hard, Tom's a good man and don't belong in here around all these criminals." Roy said then nodded at Tom. Tom was so impressed with his new friend and to Tom's surprise Charles got up to speak.

"The first time I met Tom I don't think he liked me very much, don't know if he likes me now, but I saw something in him. Tom feels like his people have been through a lot of heartache and discrimination and they have, and in some places still is and it hurts me to see people my color treat black people that way. You see Judge that beautiful black lady over there." He said pointing at his smiling wife Gloria. "That's mine and if I saw anyone treating her anyway but fair and equal, you'd have to put me up in this jail house. I said all that to say that Tom is a good man and he needs to be free to see black and white and red and whatever other color people all together loving and living together." Charles said. Tom was overwhelmed; never would he have ever thought that a white man would be standing up for him it was a humbling experience. "Is that all Mr. Owens?" "No, your honor we have one more." Then from the back Trey was led in all locked up in chains with two guards with him. Tom's heart almost stopped, seeing those chains again and remembering how they felt. Trey stood there a while looked at his mother then at Tom. "Judge I ain't gonna lie, I belong in here I committed many crimes but the biggest one I committed was to my mama. I disrespected her and I didn't turn out the way she wanted me to, and when she met Tom I could see she was digging on him, because he is a good man, but I didn't want another man running around our home. So I fought him and all along he still tried to make me see I could do better. You see Judge I never had a father around and this man was acting like one, it scared me. I didn't think I deserved it; it was my fault Tom is in trouble, that young dude was coming around to shoot me, Shoot me! And if Tom didn't go after him I would of and either him or me would have been dead now!" Trey shouted with tears in his eyes. "But the dude shot my little nephew Derrick, that's when my eyes open, lock me up let me sit here and do my time, and when I get out I'm going to go to school, get a job and make my mama proud of me. Now like I said I belong here now, but Tom doesn't he needs to be free." Trey said. Tom's eyes were moist from tears and he could hear the crying from Sara in the back. Tom looked at Trey and said. "Son you have just completed your journey to manhood." Trey smiled then was taken back to his cell.

"Before I pass judgment Mr. Brooks is there anything you like to say?" The Judge asked. Tom got up and Roy was thinking to himself "Please African don't tell them that story about how your from Africa and how you was a slave or they gonna lock your black ass back in the coo coo house for sure." "Your honor I am a very proud black man I come from a place where children honored their parents and worked hard to make their family proud where you had to prove yourself to be a man, me and my family experienced a lot of pain from the white man's hand, but today I watched how one stood up for me. And if I don't learn anything else in this new land that will be enough to know that one day that white people will change. The only thing about it is that my people have change also and I'm sad to say some have let me down. I have watched so many black people not realize that they are free in a land that has so much to offer them. I am so hungry for this, and in the past I have seen so many awful things and there was times I never thought it would get better, then I found myself here and to watch the young black kids shoot at each other and disrespect their mother, and not going to school and getting this free education, something the young slaves was denied. The young people are doing drugs and selling drugs to their own kind keeping their minds cloudy. And the black man not wanting to work, rather living off the beautiful black sister who from long time back still hasn't been freed, still a slave now to us the black man and her children.

Your honor my heart breaks to see my beautiful black sisters selling off their treasure that back in the day black men would have to fight lions and climb mountains and the white man had to steal to get. They don't know how special they are and some of that is because the black man fails to tell and treat them that way. And this jail system where the men are locked up in a new kind of slavery, but mostly their here on their own doing. My heart breaks also for the young men that instead of going through the long journey to manhood and plucking the flower their shooting pistols at little kids. I was so angry at this young man and I was acting no better than an Overseer on a plantation, so maybe I should be locked up." Tom said sadly. "No, Mr. Brooks, you are hoping for better things from our people and I can see it hurt's you to see the bad, but there is good and bad in all people, but don't stop hoping and expecting better. I heard a lot of good things about you today Mr. Brooks and since it's your first offense, I'm gonna let you go, we need more positive men like you on the outside, court dismiss!" The Judge said. "Tom you're free!" Mr. Owens said excited. Tom got up and hugged everyone that came and supported him, even Charles.

CHAPTER TWELVE

HAIL THE NEW CHIEF!

That night little Derrick recovered and was asking for Tom. Tom was so happy then went and sat with him at the hospital and told him more African stories. The next day at work Roy was telling Tom that the news people was predicting who was going to win the Presidency and that him Joe, Mo and Gary was going to Chicago for the announcement. "Come on Tom, you got to go, this is history!" Roy said all excited. Tom agreed he didn't want to miss this so after he cleared it with Charles he let his job know kissed Sara goodbye and then they all left. It took some time for Tom to get use to the airplane ride. "Wow!" Tom said as he looked out the airplane as it flew to Chicago. Then he started laughing when he thought about Obadele and how he hated climbing that mountain and now here he is in a machine that can fly him over mountains and all over the world. "Obadele if you could see me now!" Tom thought to himself.

The men arrived in Chicago got their rooms and watched the polls on TV and saw Obama was ahead. "This would be so great a black President, Hun African?" Joe asked as they sat in their rooms. "Yes from the cotton fields to the White house, wow, if Mary and Chuck could be here to witness this great day!" Tom smiled. "Who is Mary and Chuck?" Roy asked. "Some people I knew back in the day that wished for change and now it looks like it's going to start happening!" "Yeah let's head down to the gathering." Gary said. When the five men got there they saw all these people gathering together all happy looking for one thing, change. After more voting finally the announcer announced that Obama had just been elected the next President of the United States of America. It was cheers and tears all around Tom watched his friends all in tears overwhelm by the moment. "Wow, we did it, you know African when I get back home I'm gonna call Karen and ask if she would let me come back home. I now feel like I can be that man she always wanted." Roy said. Tom hugged his friend and thought already Tom could see the changes in how people got revived with hope. Then the men listen to Obama's speech and after Tom asked Joe. "How do you feel?" "You know I feel like I want to be a better man." "Me too!" Gary said then Mo said. "I just don't want us as his people to embarrass our new President."

Tom watched and listened to these fellows then told them he had to be alone to think, this was so overwhelming to him. "If the slave owners could see that this once land that they made the black slave work on would now be run by a black man, it was a exciting feeling to see, so now is this what I was suppose to see. After all that despair from the killings that tragedy of the slave ship, the plantation the whips and chains, and the cotton fields and all the hardship comes to this." Tom thought then walked the cold streets of Chicago with tears falling down his face as he thought of his Father Sekelaga. "We have a new Chief Father." Then he thought of all his slain family his younger brother Auyetoro, his best friend Obadele. He thought of his beloved mother Wesesa and how proud she was of him. He thought about Asante and how their life together was destroyed. Then when Rabbit and Lillie came across his mind and how they worked hard for the Master spending their whole lives as slaves. Tom thought about Chuck and how happy was he that he got to be free but then he felt bad for Mary who had a dream and thought if she lived in this time she could be the woman she wanted to be and wear the pretty dresses and go to school and be that teacher she wanted to be. Then thoughts of Melissa his wife came to him who couldn't ever be free to love and have a happy home with a husband and children. "If only they all could see this day." Tom said then he laid down that night thinking this is why I am here to see it will be a better life for us slaves, us Africans we will one day be free.

Tom laid down and slept a peaceful sleep. No more troubles and Trials and when he woke up he could hear the hunting dogs barking. Tom moved around and he was deep in the hole he had dug for himself after he had ran away from the plantation. "I am back, it was all a dream!" Tom said to himself getting out of the hole and now face to face with the barking dogs and the white workers. "We got you now slave, you better be glad the Overseer didn't die but when we get you back you will wish you was!" The white man said then tied Tom's hand and started dragging him back to the plantation. Then the white man noticed the look on Tom's face and asked the other white man. "Hey Jim look at that slave, he's smiling, what's wrong with him?" "Their all crazy those slaves all their good for is being slaves and that's what they will always be!" He said. Tom smiled and thought. "No slave master, one day our people will be free and we will have a black man leading the way!"

THE END. BY JANETTE A RUCKER 12 25 2008.

FROM THE AUTHOR

I'd like to dedicate this book to Barack Obama for giving me the will to write this book. I know it might sound crazy to some but, I always wondered what a slave would think and feel about how far we, as black people have gone. To finally be off the cotton fields but then to see us doing more harm to each other than the slave owners and the Overseers could ever do. After all the suffering our ancestors went through and now for us as people to not seize all these opportunities and the freedom the slaves prayed for is heartbreaking. We as people let's get it together for the slaves in our past and now for our new Chief in our future.

Edwards Brothers Malloy
Thorofare, NJ USA
May 13, 2015